WENDY McCLURE

WANDERVILLE

razOr
bill

An Imprint of Penguin Group (USA) LLC

razOr bill

A division of Penguin Young Readers Group
Published by the Penguin Group
Penguin Group (USA) LLC
345 Hudson Street
New York, New York 10014
York 10014, U.S.A.

USA / Canada / UK / Ireland / Australia / New Zealand / India / South Africa / China
Penguin.com
A Penguin Random House Company

Copyright © 2014 Penguin Group (USA) LLC

ISBN: 978-1-59514-700-4

Printed in the United States of America

1 3 5 7 9 10 8 6 4 2

For Michael

1
WHAT HAPPENED IN THE FACTORY

New York City, Lower East Side, 1904

Jack didn't notice the smoke until there was far too much of it.

It must have been creeping in under the hall door into the front workroom, where he waited between bundle runs. But there was always a little bit of haze in the air here at the factory—four lousy rooms in a tenement, really, but still they called it a *factory*. There was always dust and cigarette smoke; the garment cutters smoked more than anyone. That was what his brother said, at least. Daniel was the cutters' apprentice, and he'd gotten Jack the delivery job now that Jack was eleven and strong enough to carry a whole day's worth of piecework bundles on his back.

Daniel was sixteen and he made good money. He wore his hair slicked back under a bowler hat that he brushed clean every night.

And now it was Daniel who pushed open the hall door to the workroom, bellowing the way he did whenever Jack slept late. It took Jack a moment to realize that his brother was shouting, "*Fire!*"

"Fire in the back!" The smoke, an angry, dark bloom of it, seemed to burst through the door with Daniel. Two of the seamstresses stumbled in after him, red-eyed and gasping for breath.

Jack stood, his legs suddenly shaky.

"Where's the fire pails, Jack?" Daniel was scanning the room. "And what are *you* doing up here?"

Jack had been taking a break by the front window as usual. In the rooms where his family lived, the only two windows faced an air shaft, where there was nothing to see except brick and, occasionally, a morning cascade of slop from the chamber pots of the fifth-floor tenants. But here the window had a view and he'd watch the traffic below—peddlers' wagons and hot-corn vendors and all the fellows' bowlers bobbing along through the crowd.

Sometimes there'd even be motor carriages, black and spindly, making their way up Baxter Street.

"N-nothing," Jack stammered. He'd fetched a bundle of shirtwaists from a shop on Mott Street to be pieced, and next he had to haul some overcoats over to Orchard to be finished. "I mean, I was waiting. . . ."

Daniel wasn't listening. He spun around until he spotted the fire pails filled with water, three of them on a shelf behind the heating stove.

Jack looked back the way Daniel had come, down a corridor that was usually a dim cave. Now there was a terrible glow, with the lace curtains in tatters of flame and one of the garment racks fully ablaze. He couldn't see into the back rooms, but he could hear shouting and a wild clamor of footsteps thudding the floorboards.

Daniel shoved past him carrying two of the pails, but then he stopped at the doorway. "Cripes," he said under his breath when he saw the flames in the hall. "You'll have to help me, Jack."

Jack's mind raced. How could he possibly help? "With the pails?"

Daniel nodded. "Get that last one and wait here," he commanded. Then he headed down the hall into the smoke and disappeared into one of the back rooms.

Jack turned to grab the last of the fire pails. One of the seamstresses had already fled, but the other had stayed behind, trying to gather her things and fumbling with her workbag. It was the woman he called Mrs. Buttonhole—after her task, sewing buttonholes on shirts—and usually she was cross and officious. But now her ruddy face was white with fear as she began to stumble down the hallway.

"Boy!" she cried out. "Where's the fire escape?"

Jack realized with a sickening feeling that the fire escape was in the back. And so was the fire.

"Wait!" he cried, setting down the pail. "Take the front stairs!" He ran over to the front stairwell, which was dark and steep even when there wasn't smoke. "This way," he called out to Mrs. Buttonhole, who rushed over and began to make her way down.

"Come on, boy!" she shouted up when she reached the second floor. "The whole place is catching fire!"

But Jack was hurrying back to retrieve the last pail. *Help Daniel*, he thought.

"Jack!" His brother's voice came from down the hall. "Where are you?"

"Here!" He needed Daniel to know he hadn't

left. That he would help him. "I'm here!" Jack called out again. "I've got the water!"

By now the smoke was so dense he couldn't make out the window at the end of the hall, but somehow he found the doorway his brother had gone through. "Daniel?"

The first thing he saw was one of the wicker workbaskets nearby, which stood burning with long and rasping flames. Instinctively Jack swung the fire pail. A soft hiss rose up from the scorched basket as he doused the flames.

But it made little difference. All the smoke seemed to be coming from another fire, a bigger one. Jack couldn't even see the far end of the room he was in, but he knew there was another doorway there. And he knew that Daniel had gone through it.

Help him!

Jack needed to find another fire pail first or else he'd be no good to Daniel. He went back into the hall and turned every which way, looking for something else he could use, his eyes burning more and more with each step. As he searched in the near-dark, he would have lost his bearings completely if not for the heat he could feel coming from one direction: the back of the shop.

He kept calling his brother's name, his lungs aching with the thickness of the smoke, but the only voices he could make out were coming from below, on the second floor. "Anyone up there? The stairs won't hold!"

Jack staggered to the front room and toward the only light he could see—his window, with all of Baxter Street below. He could hear cries down on the street. "Fire! He's trapped!" They called in different languages. "*Fuoco!*" the Italian peddlers yelled.

He just needed to climb down to the sidewalk and lead the firefighters around back, where they could help his brother put out the fire. That's what Jack kept telling himself as he pulled himself through the open window and up onto the sill, barely allowing himself to relish the newfound feeling of air in his lungs. There was a ledge below—maybe he could lower himself down to it, and then to the next ledge below that, and then finally drop down to the awning on the lowest floor. Or he could jump.

No, he *had* to jump.

The fire had spread to the front room. Inside, just behind the window where he sat, the piles of fabric on the worktables were smoldering. The walls were peeling, the air turning liquid in the awful heat.

Directly below Jack's feet was the awning for the ground-floor storefront. Two stories down. Or would it be three stories he'd fall if the awning didn't hold? Either way—

Jack braced himself and pushed away from the windowsill. Away and down onto Baxter Street.

Later he could barely remember how it felt to hit the awning, which immediately collapsed like an old hammock but had broken his fall enough that he'd suffered only a scraped shin and a sore shoulder.

And then somehow after that he was on his feet. He'd searched the crowd on the sidewalk for Daniel, for his tall, thin form and his black hair so much like Jack's own. But a policeman had taken his arm and was leading him across the street, looking straight ahead the whole time.

"Where's my brother?" Jack kept asking. "My brother, Daniel."

But the officer wouldn't turn his head, not even to answer.

Sometime after Jack had been brought home, another policeman came up the stairs with the news about Daniel. The man stayed in the dark hallway and spoke to his parents across the sagging threshold of their small tenement apartment. Jack watched them from the mattress where he lay. The officer spoke too softly for him to hear, but he knew what the words were.

His mother swayed where she stood, and his father seized her arm to steady her.

"*Mein lieber Sohn*," she sobbed. "My son!"

Jack did not get up from the mattress. He flung his arm over his face and pressed it hard against his stinging eyes.

Hours later, he could still feel himself falling.

2
THE RIBBON

Breakfast, as always, was barley gruel with broth.

Frances Sweeney had a feeling she couldn't talk her way out of this place. It was the Howland Mission and Children's Home on Fifth Street, which took in "little wanderers" like herself and Harold. But, Frances thought, when you didn't have a place to stay and the weather was five below, *wandering* was just about the last thing you'd be doing. You'd get yourself somewhere fast.

Which is what Frances and her kid brother did back in February. It had been so bitterly cold out that she'd run out of nerve one night and headed to the mission and delivered to the preachers the story of her and Harold's plight. The full story, even, the one she didn't like to tell at all.

From the outside, the home looked a lot better than other places they'd stayed. When Frances and Harold had first found themselves on their own, they'd slept on pallets on the floors of one miserable apartment after another.

First they'd stayed with a neighboring family, then a gin-swigging uncle they scarcely knew, then the uncle's landlady, and then the landlady's cleaning woman, whom they hardly saw but who let the children sleep in her windowless rear tenement in exchange for chores. The stairs had been soggy, and Harold would wake up coughing his tiny lungs into a fit. They remained there until that night in February when the stove ran out of coal and even the cleaning woman seemed to have abandoned the tenement for a warmer place.

But here inside the home was a gloom of another kind. The dormitory had tall windows, but the neighboring buildings were even taller, so that the sun came in for only an hour or two at midday, making scant patches of light on the floors. The smallest kids sought out those sunny spots to play in, and even though he was seven now, sometimes Harold did, too, looking strangely angelic whenever the sunlight shone behind that red hair of his. Or so Frances thought. Otherwise, though, you never felt warm enough in the home, not even in spring.

It was April now, and Frances was itching to get out of here. She didn't want to get used to this place. She especially didn't want Harold to get used to it, either. Even if he sometimes still asked if they were ever going back to Auntie Mare's.

"I can't believe you remember that place," she said whenever he brought it up, her stomach lurching each time. "You were so young when we left." That was always her answer. Better than saying no, they weren't going back.

They didn't talk about what they were, but sometimes, when Frances read aloud to Harold from her old *Third Eclectic Reader* with the cracked spine, they would come to a poem on page eighty-eight called "The Dead Mother" and, above it, a definition: *Orphan, one whose parents are dead.* Harold never let Frances turn the page until he had read it silently to himself.

Now, before the midday meal, the children of the home lined up for Hygiene to show that they had scrubbed up. Frances didn't see the point in checking, since the soap they had to use smelled so strong it made your eyes sting. Plus, anyone with eyeballs could see how red and chapped all the kids' knuckles were from the scalding water that ran from the taps.

There appeared to be a new matron on duty today, and she was making her way down the line. She stopped in front of Frances and considered her for a moment. Frances, in turn, pondered the way the puffy mutton sleeves on the matron's dress made her look taller than she actually was. None of the other matrons were clothed as finely as this woman.

"How old are you?" she asked Frances.

Truthfully Frances had turned eleven back in March and had gone past the home's age limit. She knew she was getting old enough to work as a hired girl somewhere, but she couldn't leave Harold behind.

"Ten years old, ma'am," she replied.

The woman with the big sleeves leaned closer, as if to study her.

Frances could feel one of her braids coming loose. The older she got, the thicker and woollier her hair had become, until all she could do was plait it and pin it to her crown. Aunt Mare had sometimes called her "Saint Frances with the auburn halo" to tease her.

The woman stepped back at last. "Well," she muttered, "*this* one's a slattern."

"Pardon?" Frances said. She was used to getting scolded for her hair, but something about this matron was different. Colder.

"I wasn't *talking* to you," the woman said. And then she continued down the line.

Dinner today was stewed tripe with potatoes.

"It's beef," Frances told her brother. "Sort of." One day she'd tell him what it really was.

Sometimes after dinner, one of the mission women would stand at the head of the long tables and read aloud something from the *Youth's Companion*, which Frances wouldn't have minded just reading to herself instead of hearing some busybody drone it to death. But today one of the elderly matrons was walking up and down the benches with a basket on her arm, handing out something to every child.

"Candy?" Harold asked hopefully.

"I don't think so," said Frances. "Whatever it is, it's something silly." She got a better look and could see that each child was being given a little ribbon—blue or red. They weren't being handed out any which way, but sometimes the matron would stop and look to someone across the room, cocking her head to solicit approval. Frances turned to see who she was checking with and discovered that it was the woman with the puffy mutton sleeves on her dress— not one of the matrons, she suddenly realized, but a lady.

Frances felt a tap on her shoulder. The old matron was standing right over her now with the basket. She pressed the ribbon into Frances's palm. "Now don't you dare lose this," she said.

The ribbon was blue. Frances turned it over. There was nothing printed on it. Nothing remarkable about it at all.

"Harold," she asked, "what color did you get?" She turned to her brother, who, only moments after being given his ribbon, had scooted off the end of the bench.

"I just dropped mine," Harold whispered from under the table.

"You *dropped* it?"

"It's down here somewhere," Harold muttered. Frances could hear his shoes scuffling around.

"Pick it up," she whispered back. "Let me see what color."

Just then, the big bell at the front of the room was rung to call them to attention.

"Dear children!" the head matron called. "If you received a red ribbon, please come by the windows. Blue ribbons, you may stand at the front. Gather quickly!" All the children scrambled off the benches toward their places, but Frances hung back, waiting for her little brother, who was still scurrying around under the table.

She felt a hand at the back of her neck. "Let's not dawdle," said the old matron, steering her toward the front of the room. Frances couldn't help but notice that most of the blue ribbon holders were closer to her age than Harold's.

She heard her brother's voice behind her. "Frannie!" She turned and saw that he was holding up his ribbon. His blue ribbon. He caught up with her, and she let out a breath that she hadn't even realized she'd been holding in.

The room fell silent as the head matron stepped up to the small stage at the front of the room. Behind her was the lady with the puffed-sleeve dress, the one who'd given Frances the once-over at lunch.

"Tomorrow," announced the head matron,

"those of you who hold red ribbons will be going on a very special outing to visit the aquarium at Castle Garden."

A cheer went up from the children by the windows. Frances noticed Harold shifting his feet and looking down at the blue ribbon in his hand.

The lady with the fancy dress stepped forward. "As for those of you with a *blue* ribbon," she announced, "you are receiving a very *special* opportunity from the Society for Children's Aid and Relief. Tomorrow, you will begin your journey to your new *placements . . .*"

The woman spoke so differently on the stage from the way she had to Frances. Her voice sounded like Christmas bells practically. She was talking about placements. . . . Did that mean homes? Frances wondered. She could tell Harold had caught that word, too, from the way he'd straightened up.

". . . where you will find a *most satisfactory* situation with these kind and upstanding families," the woman continued, "in a most *wholesome* and *healthful* environment. . . ."

This lady was talking some big mouthfuls to be sure, Frances thought. All the same, Frances felt like she was floating, like the ground she stood on hardly mattered, and like she would drift up far above the tar rooftops of all the buildings whose shadows darkened the Howland Mission and Children's Home. Then Harold's hand reached for hers, and they clasped tightly.

The matron spoke up. "Miss DeHaven," she asked the woman, "won't you tell them where they're going?"

"To a better place," the woman answered. *"Kansas."*

3
PLACED OUT

Kansas, Jack thought. *Not dead, and going to Kansas.* Three weeks after he'd escaped the fate that had claimed his brother, this was his life now. It was like he was being punished for surviving.

On any other day the train shed at Grand Central Depot, a huge, arching expanse of steel and glass and soot and noise, would have been enthralling to Jack. Instead, the hugeness of it all was grim, and the platform he walked along seemed to go on forever.

In front of him was the man from the Society for Children's Aid and Relief who was leading him to the train. But Jack kept his eyes fixed on the distance ahead of them, where the tracks vanished into the tunnels at the end of the train shed. Soon he'd be disappearing into that unknown.

In the days after the fire that killed Daniel, his mother hadn't wanted Jack to leave the apartment, not even to fetch coal for the stove.

"I don't want to lose him, too," he'd heard her say to his father one night when she thought Jack was sleeping.

His father, on the other hand, ate with his coat on in the mornings and pushed himself from the table as soon as he was finished, stalking out without a word. At first it seemed he was finally looking for work again, but when he crashed through the door late at night, bringing the stale scent of beer with him, Jack knew better.

But then one morning Father stayed at the table and didn't say a word while Mother brought out Daniel's good jacket and told Jack to put it on. He pulled it over his shoulders dutifully, though it seemed his mother couldn't even look at him.

"Am I to go back to work?" he asked.

His father spoke up at last. "Not to work," he'd said. "We're having you placed out. It's for the best." It was the first thing he had said to Jack in days.

That had been a week ago. Now Jack had a new set of clothes—a black wool suit coat, trousers, and a starched shirt with a collar that felt rough as rope—and a cardboard valise. And now he knew that to be "placed out" meant you were put on a train to live with strangers out west. It was called the Children's Emigration Program, the man from the Society for Children's Aid and Relief Office had explained.

"The newspapers call them orphan trains," he'd told Jack. "But a great many of our placements are not truly orphans, just children in need of a better situation."

They might as well be orphans, Jack had thought.

Now, here in the depot, he could sense his parents walking right behind him.

Jack wiped his eyes on his sleeve. The depot felt too bright, the sun bearing down on the glass roof. He could see a dozen or more of the Emigration kids boarding a nearby train car. There was a girl whose hair was being brushed by a woman who spoke to her in Swedish or maybe Norwegian, and a boy in a knit cap who shook his head and cried as his father knelt beside him. Some of the children formed tight groups together and shuffled their steps as the Relief Society workers steered them toward the train. Others stood alone. Jack could see that a few of them were pulling at the collars of the outfits they'd been given or else were limping in their hard, new shoes.

There was a girl about Jack's age with brown hair pinned up into a crown of frizzled plaits. Her hand was clasped tightly around the hand of a little red-headed kid next to her. *Daniel would do that,* Jack thought, his breath catching in his chest.

The girl, Jack noticed, appeared to be giving Grand Central one last, hard look. After a moment, their eyes met. Maybe she was thinking the same thing he was—that the world was moving underneath their feet whether they stood still or not.

As Jack approached the train, he knew at some point he was going to have to turn back to see his parents, but he couldn't bring himself to do it just yet. They had come to see him off, and it was supposed to mean that they cared. But putting him on an orphan train when he wasn't even an orphan was somehow also supposed to mean that they cared. Daniel was dead. Jack was going to Kansas so he wouldn't wind up dead, either. Jack tried to work it all out, but it wouldn't come out even in his mind.

He would have kept on walking to the end of the platform, to the end of the earth, but the man from

the Relief Society suddenly stopped at one of the last
cars and motioned for Jack to board.

Jack climbed one of the iron steps leading up into
the coach, and then another. He braced himself to
enter the train when suddenly a sharp cry rang out
over the din of the station. His mother.

"Jack!" she shrieked. He turned around to see her,
and she grasped his hand. She looked much older
suddenly, with her eyes red and her brow crumpled.
"I can't do this," she said, her voice hoarse. Then
she clamped one hand over her mouth to keep from
crying out again.

His father turned his head away. "We mustn't
stay," he said.

Jack couldn't speak. He could only nod, his
throat burning and tight. Then he boarded the train.

4

"WELL-MANNERED CHILDREN DO NOT ASK QUESTIONS"

It started with the big blond kid stopping Frances's little brother in the aisle.

"What's your name, mick?" the kid demanded. His hair was yellow-white, and he didn't look like he had any eyebrows.

"Harold," her brother answered.

"*Hair-red?*" barked the blond kid. Behind him two other boys laughed.

Frances stood up to fetch Harold and lead him back to their seat. But by then the blond kid's friends had moved out into the aisle on either side of him, blocking Harold in. In his new coat, which was a size too big for him, Harold seemed even smaller and very much like a snail that wanted to hide in its shell.

The train had started moving, lurching with

considerably more force than the streetcars Frances was used to. The boys who were picking on Harold braced themselves against the seat backs, but poor Harold stumbled and fell down.

"Watch out, Hair-red!" one of the boys called out.

"Are you lame, Hair-red?" said the big blond one—Frances had heard his friends call him Quentin. There seemed to be something wrong with his mouth, she noticed. His top lip looked kind of smashed and curled back oddly, exposing one of his front teeth, which gave the effect of a permanent sneer.

"If you're lame, Hair-red, the folks in Kansas won't want ya," Quentin said. "They'll send you to live in the trash dump."

Harold shook his head, still crouched down in the aisle. "No . . . they won't," he said haltingly.

"Leave my brother alone!" snapped Frances, her face hot. But she was back in a corner of the car, where Quentin and his friends couldn't hear her. Or else they were just ignoring her, in her new dress that she knew looked foolish. It had a puffy, lacy bow just under her chin, which itched fiercely.

The train car was all kids, orphan-train kids, and except for two more boys who came out into the aisle to gawk, the rest didn't dare to make a move as the bullies shoved her brother back and forth.

"You sure you isn't crippled?"

"Got some real spindly legs in those breeches."

"You think he's got one of those mick tempers?"

"Quit it!" screamed Frances as she tried to push past the onlookers. She could sometimes take on an ogre like Quentin—step right in front of him and stare him down until he flinched, because big, stupid carbuncles like him didn't know how to deal with girls. But she couldn't get close enough. "Cut it out!" she cried.

"*Cut it out*," said a voice behind her, a boy's. Frances whirled around.

It was the black-haired kid she'd seen from the platform at the depot. He was wiry, with deep-set eyes. He'd been boarding the next car over and she'd wondered what his story was. Now he gave Frances a nod and jumped up over one of the bench seats. Then he launched himself straight toward Quentin.

Quentin toppled forward with the black-haired kid on his back. "Gah! Get off!" he sputtered. The kid had clamped his hands over Quentin's eyes so that he staggered blindly, arms flailing. A roar of laughter went up throughout the car. The other boys backed away, and Harold hurried over behind Frances. Finally the kid let go of Quentin's head and dropped down to his feet.

"Sorry," the boy said with a grin. "Thought you were someone else."

Maybe his escape from the fire had made Jack a little foolhardy. But after leaping two stories down into a street, Jack thought jumping on the back of some big, dumb towheaded thug was nothing. Especially after he'd seen the scared faces of some of these younger kids.

Of course, now the bully was pretty steamed. He grabbed Jack by the front of his coat and shook him. "You thought I was *what*?"

Just then, the door at the engine end of the car burst open and two women came hurrying up the aisle.

Frances could feel Harold holding onto the back of her new felt coat. "Stay where you are," she told him under her breath. She suspected most of the younger children were together in the adjacent car, but she wasn't going to leave her brother to ride with strangers. She stepped back between seats so that Harold was hidden in the space behind her. She figured the less the Relief Society women saw of him, the better.

"What on earth is going on?" one of the women called out to Quentin and the black-haired boy. She wore her hair in a loose bun and her sleeves were already pushed up, as if she'd spent the whole morning working. By Frances's reckoning, she seemed young, about as old as a new schoolteacher. With more than twenty kids to handle on this train, Frances thought, she'd better not be *too* new. Well, at least she wouldn't have to look after Harold—Frances did that job better than anybody.

As for the second woman, she stood quietly in back, but Frances recognized her right away—the lady who had come to the home, Miss DeHaven. Indeed, the sleeves of her black traveling dress had big poufs at the shoulders. On her bodice she wore a blue badge, trimmed with a ribbon frill, bearing the letters S C A & R.

Quentin had let go of the black-haired boy's coat but was still glaring at him.

"Gentlemen, *please*," the first woman said to them. "I am Mrs. Routh." She had a round face with a sweet smile, and she had to clear her throat before raising her voice. "And it is my duty to make sure you children get to Kansas without . . . well, without murdering each other!" She sighed and shook her head. "Is there a problem already?"

"He jumped on me!" Quentin yelped.

"I took him for an old buddy of mine," the black-haired boy explained.

Frances stepped forward and spoke up. "He thought he knew him from his gang . . ." The names of some of the notorious old Lower East Side gangs she'd heard about raced through her head: the Dead Rabbits, the Bowery Boys, the Plug Uglies, the Forty Thieves . . . "The Ugly Rabbits," Frances finished, winking at the boy.

Mrs. Routh sighed. "'Ugly Rabbits'?"

The black-haired boy shot Frances a grin—there was no such thing as the *Ugly* Rabbits—and went on. "Thus I greeted him in our usual scrapping fashion. Which I know is a bit rough. But clearly this fellow is man enough to take it." The boy extended his hand to Quentin and shook it. "Jack Holderman. Pleased to make your acquaintance. I'm sorry I mistook you for an Ugly Rabbit."

Quentin's eyes narrowed, but he shook Jack's hand back. Frances had to bite her lip to keep from laughing.

"Now that's settled," said Mrs. Routh, gently steering Jack and the others to their seats, "Miss DeHaven from the Society for Children's Aid and Relief and I are your guardians on this journey. It will be a long one, and it will be far better on your spirits—all of our spirits—if we're kind to one another. And patient."

"I'm hungry," whimpered a girl a few rows back. Frances wanted to hush her. If there was one thing she'd learned from orphanage life, it was that you didn't complain.

But Mrs. Routh said only, "My goodness!" and checked the watch on the chain around her neck. "No wonder we have some empty stomachs among us. It's already past one o'clock. Miss DeHaven, perhaps you can speak more to the children about what to expect while I fetch the dinner pails?"

"Of course," Miss DeHaven said with a thin smile.

Mrs. Routh went out the door to the next car. When it fell shut, the only sound was the metronome rhythm of the train, and though it swayed quite a bit, Miss DeHaven remained steady. Perfectly still, in fact. Only her face had changed. Her smile had gone flat.

"What to expect," Miss DeHaven said. "It's quite simple. *Don't* expect."

A boy sitting near Jack raised his hand.

"Put that down," she snapped. "I said don't expect. Don't expect me to answer questions. Well-mannered children do not ask questions. Don't expect to have your sticky chins wiped clean by Mrs. Routh and me, or your shoes buttoned. And when you meet your benefactors, don't expect that the pity you see in their faces will get you anywhere. It's just pity, and you should be ashamed of it."

The quiet throughout the car was punctuated only by the dull clattering of the train. Frances held her breath. At the home this woman had spoken so melodiously when she'd stood with the matrons and addressed the crowd in the dining hall, but here her voice was cool and measured—and, Frances was sure, her true manner of speaking.

"I know your kind," Miss DeHaven went on. "You have become accustomed to hardship, and that is your only virtue. It is *my* duty to keep that virtue cultivated in you for the next four days. I believe that when you get to Kansas"—she paused and scowled at two little Swedish girls sitting in a row near her—"*if* you get to Kansas, you will appreciate how well I have prepared you."

Harold had been crouched down against Frances to stay out of sight, just as she'd told him to do. She felt his little shoulders become tense with fear. Still, she didn't dare look down at him until Miss DeHaven turned her back.

"I don't want to go to Kansas!" whispered someone in the row in front of them, a tall boy named Lorenzo.

"Don't want to g*o*?" Miss DeHaven whirled back around and glared in Lorenzo's direction for a moment. Then she touched her ribboned badge and smiled sweetly.

"It doesn't matter what you want," she told the boy. She raised her voice so that everyone could hear. "It doesn't matter what *any* of you want! We know what's best." She narrowed her eyes. "And we know *better than you*."

5.
THERE ARE RUMORS

"You're all so quiet now," Mrs. Routh remarked as she walked down the aisle with a basket full of wrapped sandwiches under her arm.

She doesn't know, Jack thought. *She couldn't have heard what Miss DeHaven had said to them, could she?* Both women were in the train car now, passing out the food. At least Mrs. Routh was working his end of the car and not Miss Meansleeves. From what he could see, Miss DeHaven liked to pick up each sandwich by its corner, pinching it like she was holding the tail of some dead creature, and then drop it into a lap.

At home right about now, his mother would be setting out the dishes on the oilcloth with the flower pattern, the yellow and blue roses that were the only real color in the apartment. The potatoes and cab-bage would be too hot, and so he and Daniel would have to wait to eat them, making funny faces at each other to pass the time. Jack idly began scrunching his mouth in imitation of Daniel's best expressions.

He heard a giggle. The little redheaded kid in the row in front of him had turned around and caught Jack making faces. Jack gave him a nod and grinned at the kid—Harold, he'd overheard his sister call him. Now Harold was like a friendly puppy, the way he kept looking back at Jack.

Just then Mrs. Routh stopped at Jack's row. She handed him—gently—a sandwich wrapped in brown paper. He hadn't realized how hungry he was until his nose picked up the tang of pickles.

"Thank you," he said. And then he asked, "Ma'am, are you from Kansas?"

"I sure am," she told him. "Not far from where you're headed, in fact. My husband is the sheriff of Malcolm County, and we live in Whitmore—the county seat. That's why I volunteered to help out the Society on these trains. I figured they could use a local gal."

"Where we're going, is it . . ." He was trying to find the right words. "A nice place?"

Mrs. Routh's smile changed a little. "I hope you think it is," she said softly as she moved on to the next row.

There was no sense in completely hiding Harold from Mrs. Routh and Miss DeHaven when they were passing out food. Instead, Frances had him sit on his suitcase to look taller and older. She grabbed two sandwiches as quickly as she could and then slid back in next to Harold. When she handed him his food, she put her finger to her lips, a gesture that she had taught him to mean *be quiet like a mouse*.

But then Harold had to be a baby. "I only got half the sandwich!" he protested once he'd torn off the string and unfolded the paper wrap.

"You know how rude it is to complain," Frances said. The last thing she wanted to do was call attention to how young her brother was, maybe too young to ride in the car with the bigger kids. "I'm sure it's just a mistake," she said, unwrapping her food.

But then she saw, too: It was half of a thin cheese sandwich—a *tiny* half, the size of a twice-folded handkerchief—with a few sliced pickles. She slipped out of her seat, pulling nervously at the awful bow on her new dress. She knew it was better to just lie low. But sometimes, when Harold was hungry enough, he sure could make a scene. So Frances steeled herself and stepped down the aisle.

"Excuse me," she whispered to Mrs. Routh. "Will there be . . . uh, more?"

Mrs. Routh hesitated. "Not until tomorrow," she whispered back. Their eyes met, and Frances could sense that there was shame. The woman seemed to appreciate that Frances was keeping her voice down. Then again, Frances looked around and could see that none of the other kids wanted to say anything about the food, even though they couldn't hide the looks on their faces when they'd unfolded the thick waxed paper that made the packages look so much bigger than their contents.

"You're *welcome*," Miss DeHaven said to the silent train car.

Mrs. Routh counted the last sandwiches in her basket carefully. "I'll get these to the children in the next car." She hurried out.

Miss DeHaven looked around and, seeing that she was the lone adult in the car, passed out her few remaining sandwiches with even more haste. Then

she brushed off her dress, shuddered as if she'd finished an especially foul chore, and rushed down the
aisle in the direction Mrs. Routh had gone.

"Don't make me come back in here," she muttered to the children on her way out.

Now Frances could feel Harold trembling quietly
next to her. She scooted closer to him on the bench,
worried that at any second he'd let forth with the
tears—they were already building up in his eyes like
water in rain barrels.

"I hate pickles," she lied. "You can have all of mine."

Suddenly, Frances was startled by the sound of
another voice: "Ahem." And then a hand appeared
over the seat back, three sliced pickles in its grasp.
"I can't stand them, either," said Jack from behind
them. "You should have mine, too, Harold."

"Thank you, Frances," Harold said, sniffling a
bit. "Thank you, too, Jack."

By now Jack was leaning over the back of the seat.
"So that's your sister's name? Frances?" he asked.

Harold nodded. But Frances could see that Jack
was waiting for her to answer.

"Yes," she said, surprising herself. She hadn't
intended to tell her name to anyone else on the train.

Not just because of the kids like Quentin, who'd learn your name and then use it against you, but because of the kids who'd learn it and you wouldn't see each other again and then your name was just a useless word somewhere.

But there was Jack, whose eyes were kind. He leaned in with his elbow against the back of the seat, chin in hand, like he was ready to relax and stay awhile. His other hand reached out to shake hers.

"Yes," she said again. "I'm Frances."

Frances and Jack each gave Harold part of their sandwiches, too. Then they figured out how to move the seat backs so that their benches faced each other like a little booth. They sat there the rest of the afternoon watching the telegraph wires swoop up and down as the scenery rolled by.

"A gang called the Ugly Rabbits." Jack laughed. "That was a good one."

"So was when you rode piggyback on Quentin," Frances said. "You should have seen his face."

"Never mind Quentin. What about that Miss DeHaven?"

"I don't like her," Harold whispered. "She's the scare lady. Her badge says so."

Frances had to hold back a giggle. "The letters on her badge are *S-C-A-R*, Harold. They stand for Society for Children's Aid and Relief. You're reading them wrong."

"Well, then, the badge is wrong," Harold insisted. "Because she's *SCARY*."

"You're right about that," Jack said. "You know what I call her? Miss Meansleeves." He started humming the song "Greensleeves," and Frances and Harold couldn't stop laughing.

"I bet that's why there wasn't enough food today," Frances added. "She's hiding it all in her sleeves."

Jack snorted. "Ha! What do you think, Harold?"

Harold had turned to the window. His eyebrows were scrunched up, and he was chewing on his lip.

"What's wrong?" Frances asked.

"Remember what Quentin said about how in Kansas they wouldn't want you if you were lame?" he asked. "What did that mean?"

"You're not lame," Frances told him. "You run all over the place, silly."

"But it does make you wonder what it's going to be like in Kansas, doesn't it?" Jack pointed out. "It makes you think about the . . . the rumors."

Rumors. The word gave Frances a shivery feeling.

She'd first started hearing the rumors at the home, not long after the ribbons were handed out. The whispers went from bed to bed that night. Then, at Grand Central Depot, she'd listened to the Italian kid, Lorenzo, telling another boy stories he'd heard about what happened at the end of these train journeys.

"Is it true that when you get off the train, they make you line up so the grown-ups can pick you out?" Harold asked.

"I don't know," Jack said. His brow was furrowed, Frances noticed. *Had he heard that rumor too?*

Near dusk the train made a stop outside Harrisburg, Pennsylvania. Mrs. Routh brought in a water pail with a dipper, and everyone lined up for a drink.

Jack noticed Mrs. Routh pulling the porter aside to request the pail be refilled. "*Someone* was supposed to make sure the children weren't thirsty," she said wearily. Jack supposed she meant Miss DeHaven. "But I'll take care of it from now on. I'm here to help, after all."

Then the train continued in the direction of the sunset. It was getting dim inside the train car, with only a few of the kerosene lamps hanging from the top of the car flickering weakly. Some of the younger kids began to doze, but Jack and Frances talked on in low voices, with Harold doing his best to stay awake.

"A kid behind me in line said he'd heard when the adults are picking you out, they inspect your teeth," said Jack. "Like a horse or something."

"If someone puts their hand in *my* mouth, I'll bite them," Harold said.

"I heard they pick the strong kids for hard work, and sometimes they even send you to a factory," Frances added.

Jack's shoulders tensed at the word *factory*. A few months back it wouldn't have sounded like the worst thing. But that was only because of Daniel.

Jack lowered his voice to a whisper. "So do you think it's true about the work farm in Kansas? I overheard a kid in Quentin's bunch talking about it in the water line. Something about a cruel family who made kids sow rocks and eat dirt clods for dinner."

Frances whispered back. "You mean the one with a hundred kids? I thought that was in Ohio."

"No, Ohio is where they have the factory where they make kids paint tiny numbers on watches," Jack said. "I heard that story back in the city from a kid who I used to play stickball with whose cousin was sent on an orphan train to Ohio—something about how kids do a better job because they have smaller hands."

Harold spoke up again. "Those are just stories, right, Frances? Just like back at the home, when people used to say all kinds of crazy things and you'd tell me not to listen to them." He looked at his sister for confirmation, then continued before she could say anything. "They gave us nice clothes to wear, so I think we are going to nice homes with people who can take care of us."

Frances squeezed Harold's shoulder and looked over at Jack. She smiled a little, but not in her eyes.

"Sure," Jack said. "Nice homes."

It was dark now in the train. Just one of the lamps still flickered, and the only light outside was from a shard of the moon. Frances felt Harold's head loll on her shoulder. A few minutes later he was fast asleep.

Frances was just about to nod off herself when she heard a voice, faint but familiar.

"Frances . . . hey, Frances!"

Frances sat up with a start. Jack was leaning across the seat in her direction.

"What?" she whispered back.

"Don't tell anyone, but I'm not going to Kansas." He sat back, but he kept his gaze steady.

Frances rubbed her eyes, certain that sleep must have dulled her senses. But when she glanced back up, Jack looked as determined as ever. "What? Of course you're going."

Jack looked around to make sure nobody was listening. "Nope. I'm going to get off this train and go back to New York." He folded his arms and nodded. "And if you know what's good for you and Harold, you won't stay on this train, either."

6.
A PLACEMENT AND A PLAN

Harold had the window seat, and for most of the next two days, he kept his forehead pressed to the glass, gaping out at the fields they passed. Frances was pretty certain that he was daydreaming about a new home. Once he even pointed out a tiny clapboard farmhouse in the distance.

"Like that, Frances," Harold said. "I bet some good people live in a house like that, and we'll meet them when we get off the train."

Frances squeezed his hand and said only, "We'll see." She was glad that he was too busy gazing out the window to notice the doubt in her smile.

While Harold watched the view, Frances and Jack watched everything else.

They'd both noticed that Miss DeHaven hardly ever came into their car, preferring to stay in the next car over. Frances had overheard Mrs. Routh explaining to one of the porters that that was where the four youngest children, aged five and under, were seated.

"I'm surprised that she'd want to ride with the younger kids," Jack replied after Frances got finished telling him what she'd heard.

"She doesn't," Frances answered automatically. "That other car is a first-class coach. I peeked in this morning. It's got cushioned seats and everything."

"Hmm . . . Well, that makes more sense."

"You didn't think she suddenly had a soft spot for the little kids, did you?"

"Good point."

What Jack really wanted to talk about, though, was the plan to escape. But it was too risky to discuss during the daytime. The night before, he'd waited until most of the other kids, including Harold, were asleep, and he'd mentioned it to Frances again.

"But *how* are you going to escape?" she'd asked.

"I don't know yet," he'd said. "I just know that I ought to." His brother used to tell him he should mind whenever he "got a qualm." *You know, a sense in your guts that something's not right*, Daniel would say. And for days he'd been having a qualm about where this train was headed. "And like I said, you and Harold should, too—"

"Right, 'if we know what's good for us,'" Frances finished. "But how do *you* know what's good for us?"

Jack had wanted to say *because I'm just like you*. But Harold woke up just then needing a drink of water. The way Frances was such a mother hen to that kid was sweet and all that, Jack thought, but he wished she'd see that the best thing she could do for him would be to work on a plan to get off that train.

As for Frances, she wondered what Jack's story was. When she first saw him on the platform back at Grand Central, he'd been saying goodbye to a man and a woman—were those his parents? She'd heard that some of the children here weren't truly orphans. She'd almost asked him about it, but she stopped herself. After all, Frances tried not to think about her own situation, hers and her brother's. If she ever asked this Jack kid about his circumstances, she'd likely have to tell him about hers, and she didn't want Harold to overhear. Really, it was better to not say anything at all. And so Frances resolved to just stay quiet and keep an eye out for trouble.

Which is why, on the morning of the third day, as they traveled through Missouri, Frances straightened up and sat bolt upright the moment a stranger entered the car.

The stranger was a man. Frances sized him up quickly: older, stocky, his clothes plain but respectable, a beard with some gray in it. Honest, maybe. Or maybe not. From across the aisle, Jack cocked his head toward him, obviously noticing him, too.

Mrs. Routh had followed the man in, her hands fluttering as she tried to keep up with his long strides. "Sir, this is a private car," she told him.

"Yes," he said. "I would like to see the children." He was clutching a paper handbill. "You are showing them in Sheltonburg, yes? That is just past my stop. But I thought that as long as I was on the train, I might see if there was a suitable child."

He held out the handbill for Mrs. Routh to look at. "Hmm," she said. "I don't know if it's all right to—"

"Of *course*, sir," Miss DeHaven loudly interjected, having just appeared behind them. "All the ones here are *healthy* and intelligent."

She was speaking in that tone again, Frances noticed, the one that sounded pretty and melodic.

For the past two days she hadn't been wearing her ribboned badge, but now she had it on, pinned on her dress, neat and straight.

The bearded man was looking all around, up and down the rows. Miss DeHaven clapped her hands twice. "*Children!* This is an occasion to be *cheerful*, is it not?" A few of the kids stood up straighter and smiled. Still others sat wide-eyed, watching the man.

"Sir," Mrs. Routh said, raising her voice a bit, "perhaps we should speak in private first, sir, about your circumstances, to make sure that you're—"

"Just the *right* kind of person to give one of these poor children a home!" Miss DeHaven interrupted. "But I've no doubt you're *perfect*, and I don't see the need for formalities, do *you*, Mrs. Routh? Or . . . do they know how to do things better in *Kansas*?"

Mrs. Routh was speechless for a moment. "It's not my place to object," she said at last, nodding at Miss DeHaven's badge. "You're the authority here." Her mouth was a tight line.

Miss DeHaven turned to the man again. "Are you seeking a boy or a girl?"

"Not sure about a girl," the man told Miss DeHaven. "Maybe a sturdy boy who can do chores." He was looking over at the older boys, including

Quentin, who, Frances noticed, bowed his head to hide his bad lip.

"But the girls here are quite *capable*. Perhaps your wife might like one? They can be trained from a much younger age than boys," Miss DeHaven insisted.

Trained. Frances was fuming. Trained, like they were talking about terrier pups.

"Well . . . the missus does need some help," the man admitted.

At that, Miss DeHaven tugged on the arm of one of the two Swedish girls, Nell, who dutifully stepped out into the aisle, but not before exchanging a panicked look with her sister seated next to her. "Sweetheart," Miss DeHaven said, "please recite for this gentleman that lovely verse you know. The ladies at the orphanage tell me you won a prize for memorizing it."

Nell looked terrified, but she took a deep breath and began, in a steady voice:

> *"The little birds fly over,*
> *And oh, how sweet they sing!*
> *To tell the happy children*
> *That once again 'tis Spring.*

Here blows the warm red clover,
There peeps the violet blue;
Oh, happy little children!
God made them all for you."

When she finished, she looked straight down at her feet.

"Why, that was awful nice," the bearded man said, nodding abashedly at Nell. He turned to Miss DeHaven. "But I see she's got a sister, and I can't take them both."

Frances felt her stomach flip over. *Can't take them both.* She looked over at her brother. She and Harold were a *both*—what if someone wanted just one of them? She wouldn't let that happen. She *couldn't.*

"Very well, sir," Miss DeHaven said to the man at last.

"But what about him?" the man said. He pointed to a boy of about nine who always sat by the back door of the car. Jack had spoken to him once or twice but knew only that his name was Colin.

"Ah, yes . . ." Miss DeHaven led the man over. Once the adults had moved up the aisle, Nell and her sister embraced with relief.

Jack looked down and noticed that his own fists were clenched. His whole body, in fact, had been tense as a drawn bow, as if he'd been waiting to leap out in the aisle. As if he could run all the way to the front of this train, to the huge black engine, and make it all stop.

He looked across the aisle at Harold. The little kid must have some idea what was happening, because he had slunk down in his seat. His sister leaned over just then and squeezed his shoulder. She leaned in close to talk to Harold, but Jack could still hear her words.

"Wherever we're going," Frances told her brother, "you and I are going together."

She looked up and met Jack's eyes. *Wherever we're going*, she repeated to herself, her voice hushed.

Jack wanted to say something just then. He wanted to say he finally had a plan. Except he didn't—not yet.

Miss DeHaven was coming back down the aisle. This time, she was leading the boy from the back of the car. He had his cardboard suitcase in hand, and he was followed by Mrs. Routh and the bearded man.

"Colin is our *first* placement on this journey," Miss DeHaven announced. "And not our last."

Jack watched as Colin walked past. He was holding the handle of his suitcase so tightly, Jack noticed, that his knuckles had gone bloodless and white.

When Colin got to the end of the train car, he turned back to wave goodbye, his expression grimly brave. *He's wondering if he's going to be someone's new son now*, Jack thought, *or someone's new servant.*

The man was still walking up the aisle to the end of the car, and Jack reached out and tugged his sleeve.

"Mister?" he asked. "You need that piece of paper?" He pointed to the handbill the man was carrying and gave his most winning smile. "I could sure use it for practicing arithmetic."

The bearded man shrugged and gave it to him, then followed the others out. Jack tucked the handbill in his sleeve and looked around to see if anyone had noticed him taking it. Nobody had. Well, except for Frances.

Frances turned to her little brother. "Harold? I bet you can't count twenty barns between here and the next stop."

"I bet I *can*," Harold shot back. He turned to the window. "There's one . . . two . . ."

"Keep counting," Frances said. "I'll be back in a moment."

"Three . . . four . . . ," said Harold, not looking away from the window.

She motioned for Jack to follow her down the aisle.

"What does it say?" Jack asked as Frances smoothed out the paper a moment later. They were hiding in the train privy, which had an awful smell, but if the handbill had bad news on it, they didn't want to read it in front of Harold.

"'A company of homeless children from the East,'" she read out loud, "'will arrive at Shelton-burg, Missouri, on Friday, May 6, 1904. Come see them at the depot house.'"

"Today?" Jack said. "It's happening *today*? They're going to send us all off with strangers? I thought we were going to Whitmore, Kansas."

"Sheltonburg is the next stop," Frances realized. The train had just pulled away from the depot of the town where Colin's new life was beginning. "We're not even in Kansas yet."

"We've got to do something," Jack said. "Don't you think so?"

Frances nodded, slowly at first.

"They'll be taking us off the train, won't they?" Frances said. "I know what we can do. . . ."

"Sheltonburg!" the conductor called as the train lurched to a stop a few minutes later. Jack and Frances had only just run back to their seats from the privy.

"I counted fourteen barns," Harold told Frances.

"Good job," she said, though she was barely paying attention. Both she and Jack kept their eyes on the door to the next car.

Any moment now, Miss DeHaven would come storming in and announce that they were leaving the train. And then it would all begin to happen, turning like gears in a clock. First, she and Harold and Jack would file off with the others. But then, instead of going into the depot, she'd grab Harold and the three of them would hide in town until they could stow away on a train back east. That was the plan, at least.

But what happened instead was a stony-faced conductor came and stood at the door, as if to guard

it. Then Mrs. Routh came in, and she hurried
straight over to Nell and her sister. "Gather your
things," she told the girls. Her voice sounded hope-
ful, though she seemed to avoid looking at any of
the other children.

In a moment the two girls were following her out,
holding each other's hands tightly. The conductor
who was standing guard stepped aside to let them
through, and then they were gone.

Jack slumped in his seat.

"What's happening?" asked a boy sitting near
Jack. "Where are they going?"

Everyone crowded to the side of the car that
faced the depot. But only one of the older boys,
Lorenzo, was tall enough to see over the crowds on
the platform.

"Miss DeHaven just got off the train, dragging
the four little kids from the other car," he reported.
"And that girl Nell and her sister just joined them.
Now she's forcing a comb through their hair and
fussing with their clothes."

"So only a few of the kids are being selected
today," Jack said, low enough for just Frances to

hear. *Only a few*, he thought bitterly. A few were still too many.

Frances sighed. "Just the little ones. And those sisters, who didn't look suited for hard work."

"But they could still end up with some brute who'll make them scrub floors," Jack whispered. "Or separate them." If only he'd been able to get off the train, he thought, maybe he could have done something.

Lorenzo called out again. "They just went into the depot building. I can't see them anymore."

After that, there was no news. The train stood for a full hour at the depot. Jack picked at his fingernails, and Harold listlessly turned the pages of Frances's old *Third Reader*. Frances, meanwhile, tugged idly at the ridiculous, itchy bow on her new dress collar. She desperately wished she could get off the train and see what was happening to Nell and her sister and those other children—to see if the grown-ups who came to "select" you really looked you over like livestock, if they picked you because your hair color matched their own hair—or rejected you if it didn't. And what if some other family picked your brother but not you?

But the conductor fellow wouldn't budge from

his spot guarding the door to the train, and all Jack and Frances could do was wait.

Finally, Mrs. Routh and Miss DeHaven boarded the train again, just before the departing whistle blew. The train slid forward and soon resumed its usual motion. Mrs. Routh was quiet as she picked up the food basket and began to pass out sandwiches.

Miss DeHaven, on the other hand, was more talkative than they'd ever seen her. "Extra sandwiches this evening!" she declared as she handed them out. "That's because we found six *quite* suitable homes for your young companions in Sheltonburg."

Frances felt sick as she did the math in her head. There should have been *five* homes, one each for the four youngest children and then a fifth for Nell and her sister. Six homes meant that the sisters hadn't been allowed to stay together.

She put the sandwich in her front pocket. She wasn't hungry all of a sudden.

She looked across the aisle and guessed Jack had figured out what had happened to the Swedish girls. He'd turned his face to the window, his mouth a grim line.

Frances pulled her coat collar up and hunched down into it to hide her face.

"Why are you crying?" Harold asked her.

"I'm not," she lied. She wiped her cheek, giving him the best smile she could manage. The tears kept coming long after Harold had fallen asleep.

7.
VOICES IN THE NIGHT

A jolt hit Frances in her sleep, and she awoke with a gasp.

The train wasn't moving.

She felt another shake. "Frances, wake up!" It was Jack, his voice a rough whisper.

"What's going on?" she whispered. There were none of the usual depot noises, just the sound of the other kids sleeping.

"Shh!"

It was then that she heard footsteps—boots, she realized—and voices: Miss DeHaven and Mrs. Routh and someone else, a man.

"Who's that?" she asked Jack. The man's voice sounded stern. She could just make out the words *inspection* and *Kansas*. She gasped. "We're in Kansas?

Already?" Her eyes had started to adjust to the dark, and she could see Jack nod.

"Listen to me," he said. "We're jumping off this train! For real, now."

"What?" Frances said. *"How?"*

"Wait!" Jack whispered suddenly. "Listen."

They couldn't see the man in the dark, but Jack had heard Miss DeHaven call him *Sheriff.*

"Sheriff, everything here is in order," she'd said. "Mrs. Routh will give you the details. The children are all healthy and strong enough to work."

"Let me just see the children, ma'am," the sheriff said. Jack and Frances could hear his footfalls coming a little closer.

"Of *course.* The standard *inspection.* But it's so *very* late. I think we should just let the little dears sleep."

"Ma'am, welcome to Kansas," the sheriff said. "We're mighty thorough here."

Mrs. Routh's voice broke in. "Please just do what my husband says, Miss DeHaven. You know it's the right thing. We're just outside Whitmore, and we ought to check the children over before . . . before they're all gone."

Jack's breath caught in his chest. *Before they're all gone.* That was all he needed to hear. He looked over at Frances's stricken face.

She spoke in the faintest whisper she could manage. "I'll wake up Harold."

Jack crept out into the aisle and looked around, desperate for a plan. If they just ran out and down the iron steps, they'd be seen. And the sheriff—what would he do? He was Mrs. Routh's husband. Would he be as kind?

From the sound of the fellow's voice, it seemed to Jack that he wouldn't show as much mercy as his wife. If they ran off the train, the sheriff would chase them down. Jack was sure of it. That's what lawmen did.

Jack searched for ideas. Most of the glass lamps hanging from the ceiling had spent their kerosene, and the only other light came from the iron stove in the far corner. The spring air was still cold at night, so it was stoked with coal every evening. Jack could see the fiery glow behind the door. He had an awful flash of recollection—the flames in that room at the factory and how he'd doused them. And how it wasn't enough to save Daniel, only himself.

But now here he was, and he had another chance to do something, to help. And suddenly he had an idea.

Jack opened the door in the stove's potbelly. He picked up the water bucket—it was nearly full. He drew out the long steel water dipper and tucked it into his belt. Then he heaved the bucket backward and flung all its contents at the stove.

SSSSHHHHH!!!! The stove hissed ferociously and erupted into a huge cloud of steam, followed by the great *clang* that resulted from Jack swinging the bucket hard against the stove.

Now half the children in the car were awake, shouting and screaming.

"Uh-oh!"

"Someone's in trouble!"

"Train crash! Did the train crash?"

In the midst of the chaos staggered Mrs. Routh, who was desperately trying to turn up one of the hanging lamps. Jack looked over in time to see Frances drag Harold into the aisle. "Go!" he heard her tell her little brother, who went running into the car behind theirs. She had just enough time to shoot Jack a grin before she took off after Harold.

A voice snapped at him. *"You!"* He glanced back and saw Miss DeHaven coming down the aisle after them. He still had the dipper, so he leaped on a nearby seat and swung it at one of the lamps, which fell with a crash into the aisle at Miss DeHaven's feet. He turned and darted into the next car and down the long aisle.

He didn't look back as he ran.

"Harold," Frances started, though she was nearly out of breath. "Harold, you need to trust me." They had made it through two more cars and were standing on the rear deck of the last one. "And trusting me," she panted, "means we jump off this train."

"Right now?" Harold asked.

"No, when it's moving, silly. Yes, I mean now." She glanced back to see if anyone else had followed, but the rest of the train seemed nearly empty, save for a few bewildered passengers who had scowled at them for disturbing their sleep. Now Frances was waiting for Jack to catch up—if he even made it through the frenzy he'd created in their train car.

"But what about . . . ," Harold began. "What about the people who might come and take us? The good people?"

"With a good home?" Frances asked.

Harold nodded, his eyes full of wishes.

Her heart twisted at the sight of his face. How could she tell him about what might happen if they stayed on the train, how they might never see each other again, just like how they never again saw Aunt Mare? She had to call upon all her inner strength. "The good people will wait for us, Harold. But right now we have to get off this train."

Just then, they felt a familiar lurch. The train was about to move.

"What if they don't wait?" Harold asked. The car began to slide slowly.

"Hey!" Jack called.

Frances spun around. Jack was racing down the narrow corridor of the last car, making a considerable clamor. No—it was the boots of the sheriff running after him, though he sounded like he was at least a full car behind Jack.

"*Now!*" screamed Jack as he reached the deck.

"Help me with Harold!" Frances called. She swung over the rail of the deck and braced her legs. It was like getting off the Sixth Avenue trolley, she thought. Just . . . *bigger.* And getting faster. She landed easily and kept running alongside.

"Reach out and grab Frances!" Jack told Harold, lifting him under his arms. Before Frances knew it,

Harold was holding her, and together they tumbled to the ground. Still, they were safe.

Jack could feel the train gaining speed. "Come on!" Frances cried.

The sheriff was close enough to call to him now. "*Boy!*" he shouted. His mustache was one big dark frown. "Stay right there!"

Here I am again, Jack thought as he swung over the deck rail. It seemed that no matter how hard the world pushed, he still had to jump. His legs bent into a crouch. He looked down at his feet and saw the ground speeding by, getting faster with every moment.

"Can't stay!" he shouted. And so he jumped free.

8.
A FIELD OF NOTHING

"**K**ansas sure is dark," said Harold as the three of them walked.

They hadn't stayed to watch the train disappear. "We have to put some distance between us and the spot where we jumped," Jack had explained. So they'd run down an embankment and then headed straight away from the tracks, following the faint half-moon in the sky.

Frances's eyes couldn't make out anything in the dark except a horizon. "What's this we're walking across, a field?" she asked Jack. She was glad to have Harold clutching her hand; without it she would have felt as if she were drowning in all this night.

Jack reached down and felt rough, dry grass and hard ground. "I don't think there's anything planted out here. Just a field of nothing." Turning to Frances, he whispered, "At least we're not on someone's farmland, which means we won't get caught for trespassing."

Frances nodded, then added even more quietly, "True, but it also means there's nowhere to hide. No barn or stable or any place where we can go."

"We'll find something," Jack mumbled. He couldn't let himself give in to the feeling that maybe he shouldn't have dragged Frances and Harold off the train. "Anyway, it's so dark. Maybe no one will see us, right?"

Frances didn't say anything for a moment. "I guess," she said finally.

Truthfully, the darkness was unlike any Jack had ever seen. In the city the streets were electric-lit, but out here there weren't even any shadows, just the constant gray-black that felt heavy on his eyes like a haze. He wondered if a person could become deranged walking around in so much darkness. "You're not afraid of the dark, are you, Harold?" he asked, trying to lighten the mood.

"No," said Harold. "Just wolves."

"Wolves?" Frances began to laugh, but then her

face twisted and Jack was pretty sure she was wondering to herself the same thing he was: *Wolves. Does Kansas have them?* "Well," she said at last. "I don't see any."

Jack was the one to laugh this time. "Because, you know, we don't see anything *at all*. Except maybe that tree over there."

They hadn't given any thought to what direction they'd walk, but they found themselves making their way toward the only tree in the near distance, a crooked thing with a thick trunk.

"It's nice," Harold said when they finally reached it. He plopped down on the ground beneath it and leaned back against the trunk. By the time Frances and Jack sat down on either side of him, he was already asleep.

"I guess we'll sleep here," Jack said, idly kicking at the tree stump.

"And then what?"

"Then we walk some more in the morning?" Jack suggested. He wondered what Daniel would have done. He shrugged, pushing the memory of his brother out of his mind. If he let himself dwell on what had happened, he'd never be any good to

Frances and Harold—never be able to help them the way he should have helped Daniel back in the factory, and that would mean . . . He took a deep breath. He couldn't allow this train of thought to continue. "Maybe we'll look for food?"

"I've saved a sandwich," Frances said. "I'll give that to Harold."

She knew how to be the big sister, Jack thought. It was a lot like how Daniel had always known what to do. Why couldn't he be more like that?

"Fine, and then we'll look for more food."

"If that's a plan, it's not much better than the one we had for Sheltonburg, Missouri," Frances said.

"It *is* better," Jack shot back. "Because at least we're off the train now."

Frances folded her arms. Jack knew what she was thinking—that he hadn't a plan at all, only some chicken-headed notion that things were about to get worse. But hadn't he saved them all? Didn't that count for something?

He leaned across to look at Frances. If she'd meant to give him the silent treatment, she'd fallen asleep doing it.

Morning dew sounded pretty when you read about it in poems, but it was wretched to wake up in it, Frances thought. She tried to shake off the clammy feeling on her arms and legs. The sky was so overcast and dim that the damp grass was practically the only way she could tell it was morning.

"Cold," Harold mumbled. He was awake and huddled inside his big coat.

"That's for sure," Jack said, over from his side of the tree where he still lay on his side. Slowly he sat up and wiped the dirt from his face.

Frances fished out the cheese sandwich she'd saved and gave it to Harold, hoping that he'd quit shivering if he had some food in him. For once, she found herself craving a bite of the stuff.

Finally Harold let go of his coat and sat up straight, gobbling the sandwich down.

They all looked at one another for a moment.

"Okay," said Jack slowly. "Let's . . . find something else to eat?" He stood up and pulled Harold to his feet.

Frances stood up, too. "There's something that needs to be done first," she replied solemnly.

"Uh . . . what?" Jack asked.

"*This!*" Frances yelled, seizing the hateful lace bow at her dress collar. She yanked at it, hard; and with a few more tugs and a most satisfying ripping noise, she'd pulled it free.

"There," she said, tucking the lace into her coat pocket with a grin. "Let's go."

"Can you believe this place?" Frances exclaimed after nearly a half hour of walking. "I feel like we're lost at sea, except it's land."

Jack knew what she meant. Just days ago he'd felt small in the big train shed at Grand Central, but this tent of sky was immense in comparison. He found himself wishing that Daniel could see it.

Just then, Jack lurched forward, just barely catching himself. He felt the ground carefully with his feet, noticing that it sloped down suddenly to a grove of trees. It seemed to Jack as if the earth had a mouth, a big, jagged grin.

"A ravine," Frances murmured after Jack had found his footing. She'd read about them in one of her books. As she braced her knees to descend, she realized, in her eleven years of city living, she had never walked down a true hill before. Neither had Harold, who began stumbling forward.

"Whooaaaa!" he called out as he gained momentum. Just as he reached the foot of the slope, he tripped over a log.

"Harold!" Jack called.

Harold fell right over, making an *oof!* sound when he landed on his side.

Frances squinted.

Was it *the log* that had made the sound?

The log stood up. No, the log was a kid—a boy. "*Intruders!*" the boy yelled. "Be off!" And he was holding something, waving it—*a hatchet!*

9.
A BOY NAMED ALEXANDER

Jack kept an eye on the hatchet as he stepped forward and faced the stranger. The boy matched Jack's steps, and soon both were circling each other warily, one with a weapon in his hands and the other with a fist poised to strike.

Jack nodded toward Frances and Harold. "Leave them alone," he said to the strange boy, who seemed to be close to his own age.

The boy turned to look at Frances, who stood by with a rock in her hand, and Harold, who was wiping his nose on his sleeve. Then the kid looked back at Jack. He took a step back and slowly lowered his hatchet.

Suddenly, his face burst into a grin. "You're kids!" he exclaimed. "I've been waiting for you!"

Jack and Frances traded a look.

"*Us?*" Frances mumbled.

"Yes, *you*," the boy said. "I mean, children like you and"—he suddenly lowered his voice—"you're on your own, right? No adults with you?"

Frances hesitated, but Jack shook his head. "Nope."

The kid grinned again. "What about the sheriff? You seen him?"

"Sure," said Jack. "But we got away," he added proudly.

"Far away," Harold chimed in. "He can't find us."

Frances just shrugged. Truthfully she thought Jack and her brother ought to keep their mouths shut around Hatchet Kid. He was tall and thin and looked just slightly older than Jack and her, with light brown scraggly hair that went past his ears. He had smart-dog eyes, Frances thought—pale blue and alert and a little crooked—the kind of eyes you had to be careful around.

The boy set down the hatchet. "The name's Alexander," he said, reaching out to shake Jack's hand and then Harold's. Then he tipped an invisible hat to Frances, who half smiled and jabbed out her hand for him to shake.

"I'm Frances, and this is my brother, Harold," she said. "And you've just met Jack, who's our . . ." She hesitated. What did you call a person whom you just jumped off a train with?

"Our *friend*," Harold finished.

"Pleased to meet all of you," Alexander said. "Let me show you around."

"Around *where*?" Harold asked. Frances and Jack glanced around, wondering the same thing. The place they were in was nothing but a wooded ravine with a tiny creek running through it.

"Oh, there's plenty here . . . ," Alexander began. "But wait—what's that sound?" He stopped near Harold and listened. "It's like growling."

Harold's eyes grew wide. "Wolves?"

"No, it's coming from *you* . . . ," Alexander told him. "From your . . . *stomach*?"

Jack laughed. "I think Harold's so hungry he could *eat* a wolf," he explained.

"We all are," Frances confessed.

Jack took the boy in further as the kid nodded in understanding. This Alexander, whoever he was, seemed all right, he thought. Sure, he was a little scruffy, even for a farm kid, but maybe that's how things were in Kansas. If anything, he reminded Jack of some of the kids back home. "Ever been a newsboy?" Jack asked.

"Me?" Alexander laughed a short laugh. "A newsboy?"

Jack shrugged. "Yeah, you just make me think of them." Daniel used to say they had a rough life but they were their own masters. Alexander had that same way about him somehow, a cleverness.

"Sheesh! Me, a newsboy?" Alexander chuckled, shaking his head. "What's a newsboy do, anyway? I've no idea!" He gave a big shrug, though somehow he didn't look very confused.

Jack decided to change the subject back to their grumbling stomachs. "Maybe . . . there'd be a bite to eat at your house?" he suggested. "Just some bread maybe, and then we'd be on our way."

"Of course," said Alexander, straightening up and motioning with a flourish toward the ravine. "Follow me."

Frances figured he was going to lead them out of the ravine and to a farmhouse, where he'd sneak them some food. Instead, they went just a few yards to the edge of a creek, where Alexander suddenly crouched down and pulled aside an old blanket covered with leaves.

"Let me check the pantry cupboard," he said. Beneath the blanket was a hole, dug just deep enough to hold a battered valise, which Alexander flipped open.

"*Oh!*" Harold exclaimed when he saw the contents.

Frances tried to count it all—the stacked sardine tins, the jars containing peaches and jam, the biscuits. There was a wedge of cheese in wax and a basket of eggs, and something wrapped in butcher paper, sausage or maybe salt pork—she could smell it. They all could.

"I'm happy to share," Alexander told them.

Harold gawked, and Jack looked over at Frances.

"What are the lot of you staring for?" Alexander said. "It's time for breakfast!"

10.

"I KNOW WHERE YOU CAN FIND A HOME"

Jack had never seen anyone get a fire going as quickly as this Alexander kid. Just a minute or two between match strike and a crackling little blaze.

"So where's all this food from?" Jack asked him.

"And why do you have it out here in the woods?" Frances added.

"Oh, I liberated a few things from Whitmore," Alexander said matter-of-factly. "That's the town nearest here."

Jack and Frances exchanged another look. They still couldn't make sense of all this.

"But where do *you* live?" Harold asked.

Alexander's grin got wider. "I'll explain after we eat. How'll some eggs taste?"

The campfire was suddenly Harold's new favorite thing. He kept circling it, tossing leaves on it, poking at the kindling with sticks. "We're like vagabonds! Tramps of the road!" he cried.

We are *vagabonds*, Frances thought. But if Harold figured being homeless out in the countryside was more fun than being a little wanderer back in the slums, who was she to tell him otherwise?

"Take care you don't poke that fire out. We want to make sure the bacon and eggs cook," she told Harold. Alexander had balanced a shallow tin milk pan on a ring of rocks in the fire pit, and the fresh eggs were bubbling away slowly in the bacon fat.

"Oh, believe me, Jack and I are watching them *very* carefully," said Alexander.

Alexander set the pan on a short plank to keep their laps cool, and then they passed it around, tucking away hot mouthfuls of scrambled-eggs-and-bacon with a big spoon they all shared. Despite the odd arrangement, Frances thought it was one of the best breakfasts she'd ever had . . . even if she wasn't willing to admit it.

"I don't know how I was going to go through a whole rasher of bacon by myself," Alexander said.

"Good thing you folks decided to hop off that orphan train and come visit for a spell."

Frances paused, holding the spoon in midair. Harold sucked in his breath.

Jack cleared his throat. "Who said anything about an orphan train?"

"As a matter of fact, we were traveling with our families in a wagon," Frances declared. "A covered wagon! And we were tragically set upon by bandits and have been walking ever since."

"Bandits, my eye," Alexander said. "I can tell by the way you talk. You're Lower East Side scrappers. Straight from my old neighborhood."

Frances and Jack looked at each other. There was no fooling this kid.

"And judging from where I've been and what I've seen," Alexander continued, "you were right to escape from that train."

"You mean, the rumors . . . ," Jack started. "About the work farm . . . the hundred kids . . ."

"It's all true."

"It's called the Pratcherd Ranch, and I was there," Alexander told them as he washed the pan and spoon in the creek. The color in his face had seemed to drain as soon as he started talking about the work farm, and even now he was still a little pale. "Though it's not really a ranch, as there aren't cattle there. Or at least not any real cattle. The only herd they've got there are the farmhands—kids like us. You sleep in a bunkhouse, where the rain comes through the roof and the wind cuts through. Then they make you get up before dawn, and you work until dark. Digging up sugar beets."

"They *keep* you there at the ranch?" Jack asked. "Like a pack of mules?" He'd broken his poor neck running bundles for the shirt factory on Baxter Street, but at the end of the day, he'd had supper and his own bed and coins to spend. "How can they do that?"

"They claim the work is for our own good. That we're all low-life kids who ran in city gangs and that we need reforming. But all the Pratcherd family is doing is making themselves rich on our backs."

"They're a family?" Harold asked. "You mean they have children of their own?"

"Just a son," Alexander said. "Rutherford. He's about fourteen."

"*Rutherford Pratcherd?* That's an awful name," Frances said.

"Well, *he's* awful," Alexander muttered. He finished drying the spoon with his shirttail and tossed it into the pan with a forceful *clang*. "And mean. If he thinks you're slacking off, he'll beat you to jelly."

"So you ran away?" Jack asked. "How did you do it?"

"I stowed away on Mr. Pratcherd's buckboard wagon on a trip into town. I hid out in a load of potatoes and then crept out when he wasn't looking. Then I stayed in a livery barn in Whitmore for the night."

"When did this happen?" Frances asked. "I mean, how . . . how long have you been out here all alone?"

"That was almost two months ago," Alexander replied. "After that, I slept in chicken sheds, storm cellars, and corncribs." He nodded proudly, but he also sank down into his shoulders a bit, as if he were remembering the cold. "But then I found this place, and I'm not going back."

"The only place I'd ever go back to is New York," Jack said. "Wasn't easy there, but at least it's what I know. . . ."

Alexander looked at Frances and Harold. "What about you?" he asked them.

"I just want a home," Harold said in a small voice. "For me and my sister."

They were all quiet for a moment, with only the sound of the creek nearby.

"Well," said Alexander, "I know where you can find a home."

"Really?" Harold asked.

"It's a place run by kids. Nobody telling them what to do. Nobody getting in their way. No grown folks," Alexander continued. "After all, have adults done anything good for you?"

Harold shook his head.

"Jack? Frances? Do you trust anyone who isn't our age?"

"Not really," Jack admitted. He thought about working days on the sidewalks in the city, all those grim-faced people in black and gray coats who wouldn't step aside for anyone, not even for a boy carrying a load on his back. When he'd get home, he wouldn't even make it up the dim stairwell with his wages sometimes, not if he passed his father on his way out for the night.

"Not at all," Frances said. Any time grown people made a decision in her life, all that followed was trouble and turmoil. And half the time they probably didn't even stop to think when they were deciding something for her and Harold. Or at least Aunt Mare hadn't when she left.

"Then it's settled," Alexander said. "You're all joining me in Wanderville!"

Harold was mystified. *"Where?"*

"Wanderville is a town," Alexander said. "A town most folks can't get to, and where they can't get to *us*. And it's right here."

"Here," Frances repeated.

"There's the fountain," he said, gesturing over toward the creek. "And over there's the hotel and the mercantile. The main square is right here, but of course you've already seen that. You can see it, right?"

Jack and Frances and Harold looked all around, confused. There weren't any buildings at all—not in the wooded ravine, and not in the distance, either. All he was pointing to were trees, a clearing, and an old barrel.

"If you don't see it yet," said Alexander, "just walk around."

"Sure thing," Jack said.

Frances motioned to him and Harold. "Come on, let's go see the hotel," she said. *"Now."* She took

her little brother's arm and hurried over to the far-
thest trees, while Jack followed. Finally she stopped
and brought her voice down to a whisper.

"I think it's time for us to get out of here," she
said.

"What do you mean?" Jack whispered back.

"I mean, haven't you noticed this kid is bughouse
crazy?" Frances insisted. "There's *nothing here!*"

11.
THE TOWN YOU COULDN'T SEE

For a moment, all Jack and Harold could do was stare at Frances.

"Someone had to say it," Frances said. "Alexander's out of his mind."

"Well," Jack finally said, a little sheepishly, "this Wanderville business *does* seem a little peculiar."

"Alexander's seeing things that aren't there!" Frances shot back. "Clearly he's touched in the head. Also, he wants to start his own town. He's about twelve years old, he's got nothing but a barrel and a suitcase full of eggs, and he wants to start his own *town*."

Jack shrugged. "I don't know. I think he's been through a lot. After the hardship he's seen, anyone would be a little . . . different. But he seems like he's doing his best to survive."

Then Harold spoke up. "I like Alezzander. He's nice, and I want to stay in Wanderville."

"It's not a real town," Frances told him.

"The *food's* real," Harold said.

"Harold's got a point," Jack said. Before meeting Alexander, he hadn't known how he was going to make sure that Frances and Harold had enough to eat—or really, how they'd find food at all. "Did you see that suitcase? I noticed a sack of flour stowed in that barrel, too. He's been here for a while, through cold weather, even, and he's faring pretty well."

Frances shook her head. "We should make our way to an actual town and hide out there. I don't know what we're doing out here in the middle of the wilderness."

"But that's just it. *Alexander* knows what he's doing out here in the middle of the wilderness," Jack pointed out, surprising himself by sticking up for him. Something about what Alexander had said had gotten under his skin. "Why don't we stick around for a few days and see how it goes?"

Frances drew her mouth into a tight line. "I just don't know."

"Please?" begged Harold. "Think of how good breakfast will be tomorrow."

"Fine," she said at last. "We'll stick around." Jack could tell that she still wasn't sure, but from the way she was looking at her brother, it was clear that she was glad to see the joy on Harold's face.

Frances walked back toward the creek, where Alexander was busy covering up the valise with leaves. He looked up expectantly.

"All right," she told him. "We'll stay. But you'll have to show us everything you know about how to survive out here in the sticks of Kansas. How to build a fire, find food, stay warm—everything we need to keep living on our own. Because . . ." She paused, trying to find the words.

"Because you don't want to go back on an orphan train," Alexander finished.

Frances glanced over at Harold, who nodded. *And because at least if we're here, we're together,* she thought.

"Right," she said. "We're not going back."

Alexander grinned. "Of course I'll teach you how to survive! Surviving is my specialty."

"Then it's a deal," Jack said.

"Deal," Alexander said. "And congratulations."

"Congratulations on what?" Harold asked.

"On being the first citizens of Wanderville."

12.
WELCOME TO WANDERVILLE

According to Alexander, the town of Wanderville had only two laws.

"First, we accept all children in need of freedom," he said. He was standing on a large rock by the creek, as if it were a podium.

It was their second day as citizens. The night before, they'd gone to bed among a stand of pine trees, where the ground felt spongy-soft from all the fallen needles.

"It feels pretty nice," Jack had whispered while Harold softly snored. "I think I get why Alexander calls this part of the woods 'the hotel.'"

"I still think it's because he's odd," Frances had whispered back. Still, it was the best sleep she'd had since leaving the Children's Home.

In the morning, after a breakfast of peaches straight from the jar, Alexander and Jack and Frances rolled an old fallen tree trunk over in front of the big rock. It seemed to make a perfect bench to sit and watch whoever was on the rock. In this case, it was Alexander.

He continued reciting the first law: "Any kid who escapes from a cruel home or an orphanage or some other terrible predicament can hereby become a citizen."

He looked over expectantly at Jack and Frances, who were sitting next to Harold on the tree trunk.

"Sounds good," Frances offered.

"Agreed," said Jack.

Harold clapped. "YES PLEASE!" he shouted.

Alexander grinned and went on. "As for the second law, we should always be open to donations. . . ."

Jack looked confused. "Donations?"

Alexander cleared his throat. "Uh, gifts of food or supplies or other provisions that would be helpful to Wanderville and its citizens."

"Gifts?" Frances asked. "Gifts from who?"

"Well, sometimes the gifts aren't *given* by anyone," Alexander explained. "Sometimes the things we need just . . . present themselves. And when they *do* present themselves, we shouldn't be shy about taking them."

"Like this log?" Harold asked, patting the tree trunk they were sitting on.

"Sure!" said Alexander. "It was free for the taking, and we took it and used it to build our courthouse here." He motioned around him to the rock he stood on and to the row of "seats" on the log. "That's exactly what I mean."

Frances had to keep herself from giggling out loud. The *courthouse*? Alexander was talking his crazy talk again. Then again, at least he let you see that a "hotel" was a few scrawny pine trees and a "goods store" was a hole in the ground. Whereas the people from the Howland Mission and the Relief Society would tell you one thing and you wouldn't know until too late that it was practically a lie. The Children's Home wasn't a *home*; it was a drafty dormitory with rough beds. And the only *family* the orphan train had in store for them were some brutes called the Pratcherds.

With Alexander, Frances thought, she could decide for herself what was what, even if she didn't much feel like calling rocks and trees and creeks by fancy, made-up names.

Jack didn't mind Alexander's high-flown talk at all. His brother, Daniel, used to go on about the things he was going to buy with his wages—gold watches, boots for Jack, a tailor shop of his own. That's just what you did when things were hard: You talked *big*, if only to show you weren't licked. Their father was licked; for as long Jack could remember, the man had been taken with dreadful moods that he soused with whiskey on a daily basis. And his mother was just as beaten down. But her face would light up a bit whenever Daniel talked about his dreams. She'd sit at the table with the blue-and-yellow oilcloth and squeeze Jack's hand as they listened to Daniel at breakfast.

So Jack had listened, too—not always to the words but to the spirit of the words, because he could tell how much his older brother needed to be heard. Alexander must have been waiting weeks for someone to come through these woods and listen. Jack could tell that he'd wanted to stand on that rock for a long time.

"Sun's getting high," Alexander said. "We'd better head out."

"Head out where?" Harold asked. He had been finding rocks and arranging them in a line along the creek to make the courthouse wall.

"We're making a supply run in Whitmore," Alexander told them.

"We're going to the *town*?" Jack asked.

"The *real* town?" Frances added.

"You'll see. Come on—we'll follow the creek," Alexander said. "It's not the shortest route, but with the trees, it's the most hidden path and the easiest to follow."

Jack saw Frances hesitate a moment before she started walking. He could guess why. If they'd stayed on the train that night, they would have ended up in Whitmore. They'd escaped whatever fate awaited them there, but now they were headed right into the thick of it.

"How do you know which way is which when you're out on the prairie?" Frances asked after nearly an hour of walking along the wooded creek bank. Jack could understand why she was confused—as he looked out at the flat country that lay beyond the woods, it all just seemed like an ocean of grass to him.

"I'll show you," Alexander said. He scanned the

ground and then motioned the others over. "This is a pilot plant," he told them, pointing to a patch of weeds with wide leaves at their base. "It has yellow flowers in the summer. See how all the plants have their leaves growing in the same two directions? Those directions are north and south."

"Wow!" Harold said. "How does it do that?"

"How did you *know* that?" Jack asked.

"My pop showed me. We lived on a farm in Pennsylvania before."

"Before New York City?" Frances asked.

"Yeah," said Alexander. "Before my pop died. He worked at a mill. Died there." He had started walking again. "Then my ma and me were in the city." He kept his head down. Still, Jack could see that he wanted to say more. "But you know how it is," Alexander added finally. "Don't need to tell you."

"Right," Jack said quietly.

Frances sensed it was time to change the subject. "So, what kind of supplies are we getting?"

"Good question," Alexander said. "We're nearly out of potatoes, and we need salt pork, too. Lumber would be good if we can find some we can carry. But we've already got plenty of nails in our inventory."

"Inventory?" Jack asked.

"You have to think about what you have, as well as what you need," said Alexander. "These towns out west, they always have to keep track of the stock in their stores, since everything comes on the train. . . ."

"Like us!" exclaimed Harold, grinning.

Jack and Alexander chuckled at Harold, but Frances felt her stomach drop. If the townspeople kept track of the goods that came in on the train, then surely they'd also be counting how many children were supposed to arrive. *Does that mean that someone will be looking for us?* Perhaps Mrs. Routh's husband, the sheriff?

"See that bridge over there?" Alexander said, interrupting Frances's racing thoughts.

Ahead of them, a wooden footbridge rose above the creek, spanning the high banks. "We're going to climb up on the bank on this side of the creek, and then cross the bridge," he told them.

Frances took a deep breath. The past day and a half had been so very strange. In the woods it had all felt like make-believe—especially with this Alexander kid's talk about "Wanderville"—but soon they would be back in the real world. "And then?" she asked.

"And then we'll be in Whitmore, Kansas."

13.
THE OTHER TOWN

They all stayed close behind Alexander as they crossed the bridge into Whitmore.

"Walk calmly until we get close to something we can hide behind," Alexander instructed. "Two at a time."

"It's not a big town, is it?" Frances murmured. There were just a few dusty streets, each no more than three blocks long, beginning at the footbridge road and stopping at the railroad tracks. Still, the town's tiny size didn't do anything to make Frances less anxious.

"Depends on how you look at it," Alexander replied, shuffling along. "Whitmore's no New York City, but it has all the supplies we need." He darted behind a barn and motioned for the others to follow.

From there, they kept to the narrow alleys that ran between the streets, creeping as quietly as they could from one shed to another.

"Huh," Jack whispered. "False fronts." Most of the buildings, he realized, were one-story houses built to look as if they were two stories tall in front. But now that he was creeping along the back, the town looked much less imposing—just muddy yards, crooked lean-tos, and people's washing hung out to dry.

In the alley on the second block, Alexander waited for Frances and Harold to catch up, and then they ducked into an empty stable.

"All right," Alexander told them. "Here's how I do it. I start with the mercantile over here on Front Street, right by the depot. Never go in the store when you've already liberated goods elsewhere, because they'll be able to tell you're hiding something."

Frances's eyes narrowed as she listened.

Alexander ignored her and went on. "I always stop in here and grab some straw and stuff it at the end of my coat sleeve to plug it up." He slipped his coat off one shoulder and pulled his arm out, then pushed straw down into his sleeve as he'd described. He tucked the end of the sleeve into his jacket pocket. "See, it looks like I've still got my arm in there, but you can stash things in the empty sleeve, long as they're not too heavy."

"You mean 'donated' things, right?" Frances said with a sigh.

"Look, now," Alexander said. "This is all for a good cause."

"That doesn't make *stealing* right," she retorted.

"Well, was it stealing when George Washington's army raided the redcoat arsenals for gunpowder in Boston?" he asked.

"Yes," Frances said.

"Well, have you any better ideas? Because—" Alexander stopped suddenly and crept over to the stable's grimy window that faced Whitmore's center street. "Uh-oh," he said. His face fell and he looked a little sick.

"What's wrong?" Jack asked, joining him at the window. Frances and Harold came over as well.

"See her?" Alexander pointed to a woman standing outside the mercantile, next to a black wagon.

"She'd be hard to miss," said Jack. The woman was wearing a brocade dress and an elaborately plumed hat, both of which wouldn't have been out of place in New York.

"She looks like a *Godey's Magazine* engraving," Frances added. "Or . . ."

"Maybe not," Jack concluded. The spring wind had sent the woman's hat askew, and when she reached up to straighten it, Jack could see that her face beneath was as red and weathered as a washerwoman's.

"That's the woman whose ranch I escaped from," said Alexander. "That's Mrs. Pratcherd."

"She has a lot of feathers," Harold said.

"Does she wear that kind of finery at the farm?" Jack asked.

"Not when she's overseeing the farmhands. She likes to ride out to the fields to pick out kids who aren't digging up beets fast enough. Then she marches them through the mud to muck out the stables," Alexander said. "And see that wagon? It looks like a delivery wagon, but that's what they used to take us out to the farm after we got off the train."

Jack drew closer to the window, determined to memorize the sight of the wagon with its hard top and its windowless black sides. Just then a figure appeared around the back of the wagon—a teenage boy in a bowler hat whose face was as ruddy as the woman's. He had a coiled whip in his belt.

"There's the son," Alexander whispered. "Rutherford. Even worse than Mr. and Mrs. Pratcherd."

"What are they doing here?" Frances asked.

Alexander bent his head to see the sky out the window. "It must be around noon. They usually come into town around this time. She visits the dressmaker's, and Rutherford chews the fat with some fellow at the gun shop. I always make my trips into town earlier so that I can avoid them. But I guess we got a late start today."

"So what do we do?" Jack asked. "Just wait until they're gone?"

"Wait *here*?" Frances quivered. Jack could sense that she still didn't like being in Whitmore, and he was inclined to agree. Hiding out in some fellow's shed wasn't any better than being out in the middle of town. In some ways, it was even worse.

Harold was the only one who wasn't anxious. "We can play in here," he said. He stood on his toes and tried to reach a hat that hung high on a peg until Frances shooed him away from the wall.

"I don't know if we should stay. The Pratcherds are out there. . . ." Alexander paused, his voice changing back to a whisper. Jack couldn't help but notice that Alexander had turned a little pale. "And since they're around, it means Sheriff Routh is nearby as well."

Jack took in a quick breath. "Really?" Mrs. Routh had been nice, but that didn't mean her husband would take kindly to runaways.

"They always meet after she's done shopping," Alexander said. "The sheriff looks over the wagon, and she always asks him how many orphans are coming. . . ."

"Harold, are you all right?" Frances asked suddenly. Jack followed her line of sight to see Harold standing by the water trough, looking cold and listless. "Harold, what did you do?"

The seven-year-old had been floating bits of straw on top of the water in the horse trough and had gotten his coat sleeves wet. Now he was nearly shivering in the spring wind. "Water's cold," he said.

"We'd better go back," Alexander said. "We'll dry his coat off by the campfire." He went to the stable entrance and leaned out to see if the alley was clear. "Come on," he said, motioning to Jack and Frances and Harold.

"What about the supplies?" Jack asked.

Alexander ignored him and ducked back into the stable for just a moment. Then he came back out.

"Let's go!" he said, and took off running for the foot-bridge. Frances grabbed Harold's hand and ran, too.

Jack kept behind them all, scanning the alley to make sure nobody had seen them. He'd have to wait another day to see how it felt to swipe things from the mercantile, but he hardly minded—except that they still needed food and supplies if they were going to stay out in the ravine.

He reached the footbridge, where Frances and Harold and Alexander were waiting for him, and then they made their way down the creek bank.

As Jack walked, he couldn't help but notice something strange about Alexander's left arm, which hung in an odd way. "Is your arm all right?" he whispered.

Alexander smiled and shook his coat a bit until some straw fell out of his left coat sleeve. And then Jack saw his friend's left arm wasn't in the sleeve at all but was holding a bundle against his side. Alexander was pulling the very tricks he'd just taught them in the stable.

"Arm's just fine," Alexander whispered back. "Couldn't be better."

14.
BECOMING REAL

"Where did all that stuff come from?"

Frances couldn't believe it. There was a coil of rope, a horse blanket, a small hammer, three horseshoes, and two muslin sheets. All of it laid out on the rock by the creek bank. Somehow it had all appeared in Alexander's arms the moment they'd come back to the ravine.

"No, really," Frances demanded. "Where did it all *come* from?"

"I told you," Alexander said. "I just liberated a few things from that stable in Whitmore. Plus some sheets from a clothesline."

Jack was laughing. "This fellow is *fast* . . . ," he tried to explain to Frances. "I saw him pop back in the stable for just a second, and then—"

"He 'liberated' some stuff," Frances finished for him. Then she turned to Alexander. "You sure are clever," she said sarcastically.

"I suppose I am," said Alexander with a smirk.

"Your mug won't look too clever once I've liberated a few teeth from your head," Frances snarled. "With my *fist*."

Alexander's smirk vanished. His eyes got wide.

Frances burst out laughing. "Kidding," she said. Jack and Harold joined in, and then finally Alexander shook his head and grinned.

"Okay, you got me," he said sheepishly. "And, look, I know you don't approve of the . . . you know . . ."

"The stealing," Frances said.

"But these are things we can *use* here in our town as we build it," Alexander said.

"He's just following the second law of Wanderville," Harold pointed out. He'd picked up the horse blanket and wrapped himself in it.

"Besides, you asked me to show you everything I know about surviving," Alexander said. "And this is one of them."

"He's right, Frances," said Jack. He'd only just

now stopped glancing over his shoulder to be sure that no one—not the sheriff, not Mrs. Routh, not that Pratcherd lady—had seen them.

"Fair enough," she said. She walked over and picked up the hammer, nudging the rope with her foot. "So, Alexander the Great, what else can you show us between now and supper?"

They started with knot-tying lessons. Jack seemed to lack the patience to sit on the log bench practicing bowlines, so Alexander showed them how to get a rope looped around a tall tree branch without climbing the tree. Frances and Harold watched while Jack threw the rope and pulled it taut.

"Guess it's not too hard," Jack said. It was like when he'd help his mother loop her clothesline over the fire escape rails.

Frances was looking up at the rope. "What kind of knots would you need to tie at the end to turn that rope into a good swing?" she asked.

"Excellent question!" Alexander replied. "A few figure eights would do the trick."

"Then show me," Frances said.

Frances proved to be a quick study with the

knots. She figured it came from her needlework lessons at the orphanage. "Crochet's just a fancy kind of knotting," she said.

An hour later, everyone had tried the rope swing and agreed that Frances deserved high marks in knot-tying.

The berry-foraging lesson turned out to be a berry-foraging lecture, since it was still May and berries weren't in season yet. But Alexander still tried to give the others a few tips that were easy to remember.

"Do you like red licorice or the black kind?" Alexander asked Harold.

"Red!" Harold said. "The black licorice tastes funny."

"Well, it's sort of the opposite with berries," Alexander explained. "The black and dark purple ones are more likely to be edible than the red ones."

Jack raised his hand. "Actually, I like black licorice better. Does that mean I should look for red berries instead?"

"No, no," Alexander said. "I was just trying to illustrate a point about how it's better to look for black berries than red ones. Also, you should *never* eat white berries."

Harold raised his hand. "What about white licorice?"

"There's no such thing as white licorice," Jack said.

"There is too," Harold insisted.

Frances raised her hand. "Wait, I was practicing my knots and I wasn't paying attention. Can you repeat the part about making licorice? Do you have to boil the berries or something?"

"Never mind," Alexander sighed. "Let's just move on to building campfires."

The fire lesson didn't start off so smoothly, either.

"You can start gathering fuel over there," Alexander told Jack and Frances, pointing over to the wooded area across the creek. Then he watched as they paced back and forth around the trees, staring at the ground.

"What on earth are you looking for?" he called over to them.

"Coal," Jack called back.

"Are we going to have to dig for it or something?" Frances asked.

"Criminy!" Alexander said, laughing. "City kids."

Alexander showed them how to find flint rock in the creek.

"To start a fire," he explained. "For when we don't have matches."

Frances and Jack took turns chipping the flint against the hatchet until they'd lit the kindling that Harold had found. They all stood back to admire the blaze.

"It's beautiful," Frances whispered.

"It's just the beginning," Alexander said. "We can get some lanterns so that Wanderville will have streetlights. We'll build a lean-to against those trees over there for shelter when it rains. And then we'll set up a bridge over the creek, and a springhouse, so we can keep food cool when the weather gets warmer." He turned and looked in every direction, even up at the sky, before turning back to stare at the fire.

"When is it going to be a real town?" Harold asked.

"You know," Alexander said. "I think it's already becoming one. Look around."

They all looked. There was the courthouse, with the sitting log and rock and the wall of small stones that Harold had lined up that morning. There was the rope swing, and over by the hotel trees, Jack had

hung and knotted the muslin sheets to make hammocks. There were even nails on the trees for hanging clothes and tin cups—Frances had driven them
in with the new hammer. And then there was the
fireplace, where they were all gathered.

The place looked different than it had just that
morning, Jack realized.

It looked like more than just a campsite, Frances
thought.

Alexander was right. It was becoming a real town.

15.
THE MICE IN THE CAGE

"Hey, Alexander the Great," Jack called over from the campfire that evening. "Who 'donated' these sausages?"

Jack picked up the pan the sausages were cooking in and gave it a shake, just as Alexander had shown him. The sausages sizzled and gave off a savory-sweet fragrance, and he couldn't wait to have the drippings over corn bread at supper.

"There's a butcher's establishment on Second Street in Whitmore," Alexander said. "It's run by a fellow who likes to sit out in front of his store and read dime novels when business is slow. It seems he leaves the back door unlatched."

"Why, that's awfully nice of him," Jack said, checking the corn bread.

"Fellow has no idea how generous he's been," Alexander remarked as he stopped by the campfire. "Too bad those are the last of the sausages for now. But I have to say, Jack of All Trades, you're doing a fine job cooking them up."

"No, cook faster!" Harold called. "I'm hungry!"

"Settle down, kid," said Frances distractedly. She had taken out her book, the *Third Eclectic Reader* with the broken spine, and was looking through it. "We'll just have to wait." But Harold kept squirming in his seat on the courthouse log, so Frances scooted over next to him. She turned to a page and began to read aloud.

I will tell you the story of three little mice,
If you will KEEP STILL and LISTEN TO ME,

(Frances read a few of the words extra loud.)

Who live in a cage that's NOT very nice,
But are just as cunning as cunning can be.

As she read, Alexander came over. He sat down on the rock and listened. Harold calmed down soon enough, but Alexander seemed transfixed by the verses about the clever white mice that lived in a cage and how one escaped.

"That was sort of like school," he said when Frances was finished. "Except better, because there's no teacher to box my ears."

"I can definitely see how this would be an improvement," she said.

Alexander leaned over and peered at the pages. "I know this rhyme. But I thought all the mice escaped at the end."

"Nope!" Harold said. "Just the one."

"Maybe you're thinking of another rhyme," Frances suggested.

"No," Alexander said, puzzled. "Are you *sure* there aren't more verses?"

Just then, Jack came over with the cooking pan. "Nope," he said, laughing. "Guess that one mouse didn't bother to help the others escape."

Alexander got up suddenly and walked over to the fire. His hands hung at his sides, but Jack could see that they were balled up tight.

Frances put the book down. "Alex? Where are you going?"

But he didn't answer.

Jack set the pan aside and went over to Alexander. "Are you all right?"

The older boy had picked up a stick and was poking the coals. "It's nothing. It's just for a minute it made me think of . . ." Alexander's voice trailed off.

"The ranch," Jack finished for him. He squeezed Alexander's shoulder. "How there were other kids there, but you were the only one who escaped."

"It was awful there, Jack," Alexander said softly.

Jack nodded. "I reckon it was."

"I'm no good," Alexander continued. "Can never do things right. I'm always just daydreaming stupid things. That's why I got in trouble at school, too."

"But you're *smart*," said a voice behind them. It was Harold. He and Frances had come closer.

"It's true," Frances added.

"After all, who else would be smart enough to think up Wanderville?" Jack asked.

Alexander shrugged. "That's nothing," he said. But he was finally smiling. It was a shy kind of smile, one that made Jack wonder what it would have been like to know Alexander back in New York. Alexander could have been one of the kids playing stickball in the alley. He couldn't know for sure, but he thought that whatever sort of kid Alexander had been in the city, he was definitely different here. And maybe Jack was different, too.

"Can we eat now?" Harold asked.

The sun was getting lower over the prairie, and long shadows stretched down the slope of the ravine. They ate right out of the pans again and drank clean cold water from the tin cups that Alexander had found. Harold and Frances shared the one spoon while Alexander and Jack ate using their pocket-knives. But soon enough they all figured out that they could eat with their hands. They used the corn bread to pick up the steaming hot sausages, which made each bite even better.

"Delicious," Frances said as she wiped her chin. "I think we've invented something new."

"We'll have to go back to that butcher shop," said Jack.

"We'll need more cornmeal, too," Alexander told them. "We'll get up early tomorrow so we can get to the mercantile in Whitmore without any trouble."

The thought of going back to town made Frances stop chewing. Just a few hours before, she'd belly-ached about the idea of stealing. Now, though, she found herself wishing that they'd managed to get their provisions that morning—by whatever means necessary—so that they wouldn't have to leave the ravine.

"What if the skashers see us?" Harold asked.

"You mean the Pratcherds?" Alexander clarified. "Don't worry. We'll get to town before they do. Same with Sheriff Routh."

Just then, Jack put down his corn bread. "Say, Alex?" he asked. "Have . . . have they ever come looking for you?"

"And what about the sheriff?" Frances added. "He's got to be looking for *us*."

"I suppose he is," Alexander said. "And I'm certain he's looking for me."

They fell silent, the only sounds the rustle of the breeze through the trees and the soft cracks of the campfire.

"Well," Frances said, "he's not welcome here in Wanderville, is he?" It was the first time she'd said the name of their town out loud. *Their* town.

"No way," Alexander said. "And we'll show him."

"How?" Jack asked.

Alexander seemed to think for a moment. He took a swig from his tin cup. Then he banged it hard against the rock with a loud *clank!* He banged it again, harder. *CLANG!* Then again and again and again. *CLANG CLANK KANG!!!*

The others simply stared at him, dumbfounded. "What are you *doing*?" Jack said, though he could hardly be heard over the din.

Alexander just grinned and kept clanging. *CLANK KANK CLANG!* "On your feet, everyone!" he shouted.

Then Frances's face lit up in a grin, too. "You're sounding the alarm, aren't you? The sheriff alarm!" She jumped to her feet.

Alexander banged the cup faster. "Citizens of Wanderville!" he yelled. "This is a drill!"

16.
A PLAN OF ATTACK

In no time they'd decided on the alarm system: Bang the cup with single *clang*s if Sheriff Routh was spotted coming from west of the ravine. Double *clang*s if he was coming from the east, and triple if he was coming along the creek.

"Whoever spots him first should sound the alarm," Alexander explained. "But then we need someone to run and roust the others! Someone fast."

Frances and Jack and Alexander raced one another up the ravine slope to see who was fastest. Frances won and was designated the Roustabout. She made herself a signal flag with the discarded lace bow from her dress and waved it proudly as she ran. Then the boys scattered into different locations in the ravine to see how long it would take her to get to them. She could reach them in no time, except for Harold, who didn't understand that Frances was the Roustabout and kept running away instead.

"You can't get me, Sheriff!" he yelled at his sister.

"Harold!" Frances called. "We're playing something else."

"GO HOME, SHERIFF! NOBODY LIKES YOU!"

Jack and Alexander doubled over laughing. "At least we know what'll happen if the sheriff tries to chase Harold," Jack said.

"And if he catches me, I'll give him a bunch a' fives!" Harold shouted, punching the air with his fist.

"Fisticuffs with the sheriff?" Frances said. "*Right*, Harold."

"I've got a better idea," said Alexander. "Attack from the trees!"

Jack snapped his fingers. "Swing down with the rope! Knock him over."

"Or you can jump on his back like you did with Quentin!" Frances said. "Cover his eyes and confuse him."

And so they practiced one battle after another.

Sounding the alarm, then running through the ravine to the rope swing and the nearby trees.

"Get in your attack positions!" Alexander would call out.

Then Jack would use the rope to climb to one of the highest branches of the swing tree, and Frances found a good spot in the crook of an adjacent tree. Harold could get up almost as high as Jack by shimmying up a sapling that was too thin to hold the bigger kids but was just sturdy enough to hold his seven-year-old weight. And Alexander had used some leftover rope to rig himself a line that he could hold onto as he stood on the end of a thick branch.

Then they'd wait for Alexander to give the signal. At first he'd just do it right away, but then the more they practiced, the trickier he got. Sometimes he'd wait for minutes at a time. It was long enough for them to imagine the sheriff making his way along the ravine, looking around the campsite. They'd stare through the clearing in the fading dusk light until they could see him in their minds.

Jack tended to picture the sheriff clenching his fists and stomping his boots.

Frances always imagined the sheriff muttering to himself, saying, *Where are those blasted orphans?*

Harold had never seen the sheriff up close, but he figured he would be carrying a big net, and thought about how they would take the net away from him and maybe even trap him in it or something.

Alexander just imagined the sheriff's eyes. How they would look all around and see Wanderville, see everything that had been built. And then the sheriff would stop to wonder, and he'd look up, and then—

"*Attack!!!!!*" Alexander yelled.

That was the signal for Wanderville to take action. For the citizens to swing down from the trees, or beat the tin-cup alarms to scare off the trespasser, or throw down rocks and sticks.

"Got him!" Harold shouted during their last drill. "I shot an arrow in his arm!"

"Hold your fire," Jack called as he swung down on the rope. "I'm coming in!"

Frances was already on the ground, laughing and kicking at the imaginary sheriff. "We've got him licked!"

"We sure do," Alexander said. "That last fight was amazing."

"Let's practice another one," Jack said.

"I don't know. Harold looks really tired," Frances said. Her little brother was yawning up in his tree perch. "Come down before you fall both asleep and out of that tree," she told him. The night sky had been light enough for them to keep playing long after sunset, but the campfire was getting dim.

"I suppose it *is* time for bed," Alexander agreed. "We do have to start out early for tomorrow's trip to Whitmore, after all." He tossed dirt on the campfire to fully extinguish it. "Lights out, everyone."

With that, Harold and Jack each curled up in one of the hammocks Jack had pulled up, Frances settled into the soft patch of ground under the hotel pines, and Alexander assumed his usual spot on the sloping ground.

Frances attempted to close her eyes, inhaling the sweet, smoky trace of the fire and listening to the hushing noise of the big tree in the light breeze. Just as she was about to nod off, she heard her brother rustle.

"Hey, Frances," he whispered in the dark.

"Yes, Harold. What is it?"

"Can Wanderville be our home?"

Nobody said anything for a moment. Frances took a breath as if to speak, but then she looked over at Alexander, who raised his head expectantly, and then at Jack, a silhouette in his hammock. Frances could just make out that he was grinning.

"Buddy," Jack said, his voice soft but clear, "it already is."

17.
THE LIBERATION OF MERCHANDISE

Jack read the sign again in the morning sun: WHIT-MORE MERCANTILE. It hung over the front porch of a batten-and-boarded building on Front Street.

They had just devised their plan for "liberating" goods. Jack and Alexander would go in first. Then, a moment later, Frances.

"Ready?" Alexander asked the group.

"Ready as I'll ever be," Jack said, his hands shoved into his pockets to keep from fidgeting. He couldn't help but wonder what he'd be putting in those pockets in just a few moments.

"Wait, what about me?" Harold asked at the very last moment. "What's my job?"

Alexander looked at Frances. "I figured he could stand guard outside the store."

"Outside by *himself*?" Frances asked.

"I can do it," Harold protested.

"You have to stand in *one place*," Frances told him. She turned to Alexander. "Sometimes he hasn't the patience," she said. The truth was, she hated to let Harold out of her sight at all. Once she'd had him wait on a corner in the Bowery while she dashed across the street to buy them apples, and by the time she'd returned, he'd ventured halfway up the stairs to the elevated train in an attempt to make friends with a pigeon.

"I think Harold understands that it's a big job," Alexander said. "And he's going to have to learn to fend for himself one of these days. Cross the street on his own and all that."

"I'm brave!" Harold insisted. "Just like Alezzander. He's not scared of anything. Right?"

Frances gazed expectantly at Alexander, waiting for him to respond. He had the same look about him that he'd had the day before in the stable, when he was talking about the sheriff.

"Right, Alezzander?" Harold asked again.

"*Right*," Alexander said. "Nothing to worry about! Really, Frances, Harold will be fine."

"If you say so," Frances said finally.

She stood with Harold in front of the mercantile while Jack and Alex went inside, her stomach feeling ice cold.

"Stay right here. If you see the Pratcherds or the sheriff, come in and tell us," she whispered to Harold, hoping her voice didn't sound too shaky. She gave his shoulder a squeeze. "Wait right here for Mother, Freddy," she said in a much louder voice. "I'm going in the store for just a spell."

The storekeeper sighed. "May I be of assistance, son?" His bored voice made it clear that he would not be of much assistance at all.

Jack scratched his head. "Uh . . . what kind of sweets are those red ones?" He pointed to some dusty-looking hard candies in a jar by the counter.

"That would be sarsaparilla," said the man, who couldn't be bothered to put down his newspaper.

"Oh," said Jack. "Do you have . . ." His voice trailed off as he tried to think. Alexander had disappeared into the dim back of the store, down an aisle lined with barrels and piles of grain sacks and a rack of brooms. The plan was for Frances and Jack to work the front of the store, while Alexander took care of the dry goods. He was hoping to smuggle out a whole sack of cornmeal under his coat.

Meanwhile, Frances was standing near a high counter pretending to admire a display of tinned beans stacked in a pyramid formation. Jack couldn't tell whether she'd nabbed anything yet.

The store fellow seemed to hardly care that Jack hadn't finished his question, but he persisted. "Do you have . . . other kinds of sarsaparilla?" Jack asked.

"What kinds?" muttered the man, who still hadn't put down his paper.

"Hmm, I don't know," said Jack. "Maybe . . . green sarsaparilla?"

The man just shook his head and kept reading. The man seemed dedicated to ignoring Jack now, which wasn't quite the plan, since Jack was supposed to be distracting him. Either way, the fellow paid no attention to him. Or to Frances—who, Jack noticed, was presently tucking a packet of oyster crackers into her coat pocket.

She caught his glance and smiled, a wild look in her eye. She might not have approved of Alexander's notions about "donations," but she sure looked like she was having fun now. As she stepped closer, he could see the handles of three spoons sticking out the top of one of her high-buttoned shoes.

"Pleasant day, isn't it?" she said to Jack.

He nodded and took a deep breath and headed toward the middle of the store. That was his signal to start "liberating" goods.

As he stood contemplating a row of canned beans, he could hear Frances behind him trying to distract the storekeeper now that they'd switched roles. "Pardon me, mister, but do you have any calico patterns with sprigs on them?" she asked.

"Eh, they've all got sprigs," the man grumbled.

Jack's fingers closed around the first tin, and he whisked it into his pocket. *Simple.* He couldn't believe how simple. He turned and saw Alexander watching him from the back, making just the slightest nod in his direction. Jack felt a strange soaring that was not unlike swinging down from the high branch on the rope swing.

Jack reached out again and again and took.

Nothing was happening, Harold thought. Nobody was coming. What could he do? He could cross the street, he thought. In fact, Alexander had *said* that he, Harold, was going to have to learn to cross the street by himself. Yes, Harold thought, he could do that now. There was nobody coming, after all.

Harold wished that it wasn't such an easy street to cross, to be honest; he was really old enough, and if he'd been in New York, he would have crossed much busier streets, with all kinds of carriages going by. This street was boring, Harold thought as he went right across.

He saw a building with a sign that said LIVERY. He wasn't sure what that was, but it sounded pretty close to *lively*, which was something this street could definitely stand to be more of. But when he got to the building, all he saw were horses. So then he walked until he got to the corner, and then he decided to turn the corner.

He heard a voice calling to him. A lady's voice. "Little boy? Is everything all right?"

Harold turned and saw a woman on the porch of a yellow house. She seemed kind and vaguely familiar, with a round face and a pretty watch on a chain around her neck. She was holding a pitcher of something to drink, and there was a table all set with a pie on it.

"You look thirsty," she said. "Can I pour you some lemonade?"

Harold nodded. Never had something been so welcome.

The lemonade was sweet and cold and delicious, of course, but he realized that the welcome feeling was because he'd seen the lady before. He remembered her watch. She was from the train! The *nice* lady, not the one with the SCARE badge.

"What's your name?" she asked.

Frances said he should tell strangers his name was Freddy. But this lady wasn't really a stranger. "Harold," he said.

The lady furrowed her brow. "How old are you, Harold? And how did you . . . *get* here?"

It suddenly occurred to Harold that if *he* recognized *her*, then *she* might recognize *him*. *Uh-oh.*

"Was it on a train?" she asked gently.

"Um, I don't know," he said. He took another sip of lemonade.

And then the door to the yellow house opened and the lady's husband came out. He had a long mustache like a frown.

"Where are your parents?" the man asked Harold.

But Harold wouldn't answer. He was looking

at something on the man's shirt. At first, the thing reminded Harold of Christmas because it was a star, a shiny one with five points, and so it seemed kind of jolly. But then he remembered what it meant when a man had a shiny star badge on his shirt.

It meant *sheriff.*

18.
WHAT HAPPENED TO HAROLD

You can get ham in a can! Jack couldn't believe it. And now he had three cans in his coat pocket. Plus two tins of beans and some Diamond brand matches stuffed in the top of his shoe. The soaring feeling continued as Jack stepped out of the store. It was sort of like the days he'd get paid at the factory, when he'd always get an itch to go spend it. This was like scratching the itch, only better. He couldn't wait to talk to Frances, because he was sure she had the feeling, too.

But instead she looked frantic. "Where's Harold?" she whispered. "He's not here!" She paced up and down the sidewalk in front of the store. By the time Alexander came out from the store, Frances was pale and Jack was uneasy.

"He's not here!" she said again.

"Maybe he just wandered down the street," Alexander said, trying to keep his voice calm. He tried to keep pace with Frances as she strode along the sidewalk. "You said that sometimes he just doesn't stay still, so he could have—"

Frances stopped short and grabbed Alexander's arm. "Look," she whispered. "Oh, no."

There, across the street, was the Pratcherds' black wagon.

Jack caught up with Alexander and Frances, but he stopped, too, when he saw the wagon.

"Do you think . . . ?" he asked Frances.

Her eyes were big and anguished. "We have to see," she whispered. She darted behind a nearby horse-cart. The two boys followed her, and then they all crept slowly around it to get a closer look across the street.

Alexander looked first and took a sharp, quick breath. Jack and Frances peered around next and saw why: There was Mrs. Pratcherd, talking to the sheriff and another woman.

"Mrs. Routh," Jack whispered under his breath. The woman from the train—the one who wasn't cruel. But she was married to the sheriff. And she would recognize him and Frances. And Harold, too, wherever he was.

Frances grabbed his sleeve as she took another step beyond the cart they were hiding behind, and another. She was still trying to get a closer look at the wagon, which had no windows, except for one in the back. . . .

And that was where they saw Harold. He saw them, too, and he pressed his palms against the glass. *Help*, he mouthed, his eyes wide.

Frances clasped a hand to her mouth, but a sound still escaped: a hoarse, desperate shriek.

Jack seemed to feel his own blood rushing cold and swift as Mrs. Pratcherd glanced up. And Mrs. Routh saw them, too, and then the sheriff, who looked Jack in the eye and then gazed right past him to Alexander. The sheriff's face was hard as he stepped in their direction.

He heard Alexander behind him. *"Run!"*

Frances didn't move for a second.

"Come on!" Jack said. He grabbed a handful of her coat and yanked it.

"Harold . . . ," she gasped as she began to stagger into a run.

"We'll be no good to him if we're caught. Come

on!" The last thing Jack wanted was for Frances to wind up in that wagon, too. He couldn't let anyone else disappear.

Then they were off, following Alexander through the alleys, with the sheriff behind them.

When they crossed the bridge this time, Jack saw Alexander head straight into the woods instead of clambering down the creek bank, and he managed to catch Frances's arm and pull her toward the detour.

"Where are we going?" she cried.

"Following Alexander into the woods," Jack managed to say, though he was nearly out of breath. "If we went along the creek—"

Frances suddenly understood. "We'd be leading the sheriff right to Wanderville," she finished.

Taking the woods was the longer route, but it was easier to lose the sheriff there. The three ran so hard their breathing was ragged. Once, when they stopped to gasp a mouthful of air, they could hear Sheriff Routh crashing through the leaves behind them.

"We've got to keep running," Jack said, panting hard.

He again picked up the pace, the heavy cans in his pockets knocking against his rib cage.

Suddenly, he had an idea.

He stopped midrun and put a finger to his lips. Then he turned and threw one of the heavy cans as far as he could into the woods in another direction from the one they were headed. After a moment he threw the second can. They could hear the first one thud and roll through the leaves. The second one hit a small branch with a loud crack.

For a moment nothing happened. And then they heard the sheriff's clumsy footfalls head in the direction where Jack had thrown the cans.

"He thinks we went that way," Jack whispered.

The three walked as quietly as they could until they found a branch of the creek and crouched down out of sight against the bank.

Alexander's shoulders slumped in relief. "We lost him," he said. "We—"

"Shh!" Frances said. "Listen."

It was the sheriff's voice, far away but still in the woods. A thin echo rang with each word.

"*I know you can hear me,*" he called. "*I'll get you soon enough!*"

They didn't hear the voice after that. But they had every reason to believe the words were true.

19.
ONLY THREE RETURN

When they returned to Wanderville, nobody wanted to talk about what had happened.

Alexander went straight to his tree perch near the rope swing. Jack grabbed the hatchet and went over to the campfire, and Frances sat on the courthouse log staring intently at the rows of rocks her little brother had lined up.

Jack picked up the flint and began to work on it with the hatchet. They had matches for lighting a fire, of course, but he needed to occupy himself and he was glad to have a reason to hit hard things against each other. His brain felt hot, and he could hear a dull roar in his mind. He couldn't save Harold and he couldn't save Daniel and he couldn't control the fire, but maybe if he kept hitting flint on steel, something would happen. When he nicked his thumb on the hatchet, he hardly felt it.

Tchitch! Tchitch! went the sound of the flint.

Why doesn't Jack just use the stupid matches he swiped? Frances wondered. To her the *Tchitch! Tchitch!* sounded like an endless reprimand, one she deserved to hear. She couldn't believe she'd let Harold get caught. Or that she'd let herself get carried away. She knew she should have stayed outside the mercantile, held Harold's hand instead of snatching up things with her own.

She pulled the stolen things out of her pockets and shoe tops and tossed them on the ground. Crumpled parcels of crackers. Bent cheap spoons. It hadn't been worth it.

Tchitch! Tchitch! Tchitch!

Jack was sweating from his efforts. Nearly ten minutes now and the hatchet had made only a tiny spark that barely managed to singe the tinder. *Tchitch!* All Jack wanted was for *one* thing to turn out right today. *Tchitch! Tchitch!*

He hit the flint harder and harder.

"Jack." Alexander had come over to the campfire. "Let me do it, all right?"

Jack sighed and set the hatchet down.

"Don't bother," Frances muttered just loud enough for the boys to hear.

"What?" said Alexander.

"I said *don't bother*!" she shouted suddenly. She was on her feet now, marching over to Alexander. "Don't act like you can *fix* things! You've ruined everything!"

Alexander straightened and glared at Frances. "What are you talking about?"

"It's your fault Harold got caught!" she said, circling him. "It was *your* idea to let him stand guard! We should never have stayed here."

"Well, why didn't *you* offer to stand guard?" Alexander fired back. "Since *you* were the one who was so high-minded about not stealing . . ."

Frances tried to lunge at Alexander, but Jack stepped in her path.

"Quit it now!" Jack yelled. "Both of you! There's no changing what happened! Go saw your timber if all you're going to do is blame each other."

Frances stepped back from Jack with a shove, but

she seemed to calm down a little. "I just want to get my little brother back," she said.

"All right. So what do we do now?" Jack asked. He and Frances looked over at Alexander.

"What we do now is . . . ," Alexander began. He paused and took a deep breath. "Well, we can't go back to Whitmore, because the sheriff will find us. And we can't go to the ranch, because Mrs. Pratcherd saw us. And, well, I mean, there really aren't enough of us for a rescue party. . . ."

Frances raised her eyebrows. "There aren't?"

"Just think about all the cowboy stories where they round up a posse, which is at least twenty cowboys." Alexander was talking very quickly now. "When we get more kids here in Wanderville, then we can—"

"What?" Frances cried. "This isn't some cowboy story! This is my little brother we're taking about!"

"I know," Alexander said. "I just . . ."

"You just *give up*, right?" Frances shouted. "You act like you're so brave when you talk about defending this place, but when something real happens— something bad—you just shrug? You think we should just *wait* until someone else shows up and hope that they'll help us?"

"Don't forget that I helped *you*," Alexander said, looking at both Frances and Jack. "You never would have made it out here on your own if it hadn't been for me." His eyes met Frances's and he stared hard until she looked down. "You know that's the truth!"

"That's not the point," Jack said. "You said the other night that we were all together here. Here in Wanderville."

Frances nodded. "Our home," she said.

Alexander said nothing for a minute. He walked over to the sitting log and shoved it with his foot.

"I don't know who I was fooling," he said. "I wasn't smart to think up Wanderville. I was lonesome. When I was at the ranch, it felt just like when my pop worked at the mill until he died—and I didn't want that to happen to me. That's what made me want to leave. I escaped, and it was bad out here at first. It was all I could do to not die from the cold. So I imagined a place for myself. Not just a house—where you sleep where you're told and eat what they give you, and you're still not anyone—but a town." His voice wobbled a little. "And then it seemed like once I thought that up, I could think up anything. Reasons for stealing, for instance. I know that's not exactly what the word *liberating* means."

"It means 'to free,'" Jack broke in. "It means having liberty. That's why we're in Wanderville, right? We want to be on our own and not beholden to anyone who treats us as nothing more than mouths to feed." He had begun to pace back and forth between the big rock and the sitting log. "Or . . . or mules to be trained. We're not wicked or wretched or dumb. We're not to be pitied or reformed or sent off, placed out like the rubbish, just because we're kids! Like we're not yet people somehow. Like we're nothing but little shadows who work and work. But we're not! Not any of us . . . and not Harold."

He stopped, suddenly self-conscious. But Alexander was nodding, and Frances's eyes were shining. They both looked to him as if to say *go on.*

"Which is why we won't stand to have him taken away," Jack continued. "We've got to liberate Harold."

"You mean . . . rescue him?" Frances's eyes were brimming with tears.

"Yes," said Jack. "Rescue him. And I know just how we're going to do it."

20.
A DIFFERENT KIND OF SCARED

Mornings happened at night in this place. It was still dark when they made you get up and work. Maybe it would get better.

Harold wasn't afraid of the dark, so he was okay. It was just that when he had to line up with the other kids, waiting and silent in the gnawing cold, he felt a different kind of scared. He felt it from the others.

He knew some of them from the train—there was Lorenzo and the boy with the knit cap and a girl who was Frances's age and other familiar kids. There were faces he didn't know, too—had they come on other trains? Wherever they'd arrived from, they all had to go out and drag heavy things along the ground to make rows in the dirt. He hoped they didn't have to do that *every* day. In fact, he was sure there would be a day here when they would all play quietly just like Sundays at the orphanage. And the orphanage hadn't been bad, either, had it? He was tired, so he couldn't remember.

He wondered where the lady from the train was. The nice one who had given him lemonade yesterday.

"Are you lost?" she'd asked him. "Where did you come from?"

Harold had kept his mouth shut because the sheriff was right there, and of course he couldn't say he was from Wanderville. But the nice lady kept asking questions.

"Do you live with the Pratcherds?" she'd asked.

That was when Harold slipped up and opened his mouth. "You mean, on the ranch?" he said. As soon as he'd spoken, he knew it was a mistake.

"Another runaway!" the sheriff had said.

And that was how Harold wound up in the back of the big black wagon. Now he was at the ranch, the place with the hundred children all being made to work and work and work.

But maybe they were almost done with all the work.

Harold didn't know if there were truly a *hundred* children. There were about a dozen from his train, and then there were kids who had been here longer, and they were hard to count because they kept their heads down and you couldn't tell them apart. Some- times, Harold thought, it was like some kids weren't even there—their clothes were the same color as the dirt outside, and they were like ghosts.

He wondered how long you had to be here before you became like a ghost.

The bunkhouse was long and narrow like a train car, except with only a couple of windows, and instead of benches there were beds built against the walls, with straw pallets. Each bed had only a single scratchy blanket that you had to fold in the morn- ing, or else. Harold was pretty sure that Rutherford Pratcherd was in charge of the *or else* part. The sun had come up over the field, but Harold and the other kids had to keep working. And when the day got warmer, they kept working still, dragging the tillers to make row after row and picking out stones from the dirt.

"What do they grow here?" Harold asked Lorenzo, who worked next to him with a rake.

"Sugar beets," Lorenzo whispered. "They look like dirt clods. We dig them up and then they get sent off to be made into sugar."

Harold's eyes widened. "Real sugar? How does it taste?"

Lorenzo shook his head. "Who knows? All they ever give us to eat are potatoes. Boiled potatoes and bread."

Harold was sure they'd get to have some of the sugar once all the work was done. He was just about to say so when a dull clang came from a bell in the bunkhouse yard. Lorenzo dropped his rake and ran over to the yard. Harold followed. At first he hoped it was time for dinner, but then he saw that the other children were only lining up for a chance to drink from a dipper at a water barrel.

Next to the barrel stood a man, a great big hulking man who leaned on a cane. He had the same lantern jaw as Rutherford, and Harold wondered if they were related. He found out soon enough.

"Don't you think you ought to thank Mr. Pratcherd here for those extra drinks of water you took?" Rutherford bellowed. *"Don't you?"*

The line in front of Harold fell apart as the other kids stepped back in fear. Harold stepped back, too. Who was he yelling at?

"You hare-lipped chump," Rutherford went on, and suddenly Harold could see who the unlucky kid was: *Quentin*, the bully from the train. Now he was the one being pushed around. He was backing away from Rutherford, stammering apologies.

"Honest, I'm sorry," Quentin said, his eyes desperate, searching the faces of the other kids, who were silent.

Mr. Pratcherd held out his cane. Rutherford grabbed it, and in one swift motion he turned and struck Quentin across the legs. Quentin stumbled and fell on his face. "Augh!"

He began to get up, but Rutherford planted a foot in his side and shoved him over hard, then kicked him twice. "Apology accepted," Rutherford said, a sneer in his voice. He handed the cane back to Mr. Pratcherd.

"Got to teach these ungrateful kids," Mr. Pratcherd said. Then the two of them walked off across the yard toward a big house in the distance, a fancy one with a tower.

Lorenzo and one of the other boys from the train hurried over to the water barrel and grabbed the dipper. "Rutherford's going to send us back into the fields," Lorenzo said. "Get a drink, quick."

But Harold didn't move a step, because he couldn't take his eyes off Quentin, who'd managed to drag himself to the side of the bunkhouse. Quentin slouched against the wall and tried to stanch his bloody nose with his dirty shirt cuff. Harold had been terrified of Quentin just a few days ago, but it was nothing compared with what he felt now. That different kind of scared.

Nobody was helping Quentin, but someone should, Harold thought. Maybe the nice lady. Didn't she live around here?

"Where is the lady from the train?" Harold asked the boys at the water barrel.

"Who?" Lorenzo asked. "What lady?"

"The one who had lemonade. The nice one."

The boys just stared at Harold. Lorenzo let out a short laugh that sounded more like a sigh.

"What are you talking about?" the other boy said. "There isn't anyone in this place who's *nice* to us."

21.
STRANGERS AT THE DEPOT

Whitmore Mercantile was usually the first store on Front Street to open on weekdays. Mr. Conklin, the proprietor, swept the store floors first thing in the morning instead of at closing time in order to clean up any sugar or oats or cornmeal scattered in the night by vermin. *Better rats and mice than those thieving kids*, he thought.

As he stepped out onto the front porch and continued sweeping, the windows began to rattle. It was just after nine in the morning, and there was a train due, its hollow whistle sounding in the distance. Mr. Conklin looked up and glanced across the street at the depot. Was there someone on the platform? He thought he'd seen movement out of the corner of his eye, but the depot was deserted.

He might have gotten a closer look had it not been for the train, which pulled in just then in a tumult of smoke and noise and slid to a stop. The town seemed to wake up with the train's arrival. A few vehicles were now making their way along Front Street—the postmaster, a livery coach, the Pratcherd wagon. The mercantile would have customers soon. Mr. Conklin finished sweeping and went inside.

The train slid away, leaving three figures on the platform: a girl and two boys around the ages of eleven or twelve. Nobody seemed to notice them.

"Look around," Jack whispered to Frances and Alexander. "Act like we just got off the train."

"I'm acting as natural as I can," Frances said.

So far, Jack's plan had gotten them into town unnoticed. That had been Step One. The three of them had set out at the first light of morning. They'd made their way to Whitmore by crossing the prairie instead of following the creek, since Jack suspected the sheriff would be looking for them in the woods where he'd chased them before. When they reached the depot, they hid nearby and waited. The commotion of the morning train had been a perfect distraction, letting them slip into town in plain sight.

It was all going smoothly enough. Alexander, though, kept glancing around in every direction as they crossed Front Street and found the alley.

Suddenly he stopped. "I'll be back," he told Jack and Frances. He turned sharply and disappeared down one of the other side streets.

"Wait!" Jack whispered after him.

Frances tugged Jack's arm. "But it's better if the three of us aren't seen walking together, right? Now it's just two of us out here."

"I suppose," Jack said. He kept walking and tried to breathe normally. "Let's just go to the waiting place." They'd decided—no, *he'd* decided—to hide out in the empty stable behind Second Street until it was time for action, for Step Two. It had seemed simple enough the night before, back in Wanderville, when Jack told the others his plan. Now, though, he was so anxious he could almost hear his own heartbeat in his ears. It kept pounding as he found the stable and darted inside behind Frances.

Jack's eyes strained to adjust to the dark. One of the horse stalls appeared to be occupied, but otherwise the stable was just as they'd left it three days ago.

Frances was tiptoeing over to the stall. "Hello?" she said.

"Are you talking to a *horse*?" Jack said.

"Of *course*," said the horse.

"Augh!" said Jack.

"Gaah!" said Frances.

But it wasn't a horse; it was Alexander. He came out of the stall holding two big loaves of bread.

"You scared us half to death!" Frances said. "Why did you disappear like that?"

"I figured I'd stop by the bakery to liberate some bread that we could eat while we were waiting for Step Two," Alexander said. He tore off hunks of bread and handed them to Frances and Jack. "I assumed it'll be a while."

"I wouldn't be so sure," Jack said. He nodded in the direction of the window. "I think Step Two just stepped out."

They looked out and saw Rutherford Pratcherd across the street, pacing back and forth along the wooden sidewalk in a pair of new boots. He paused to look at his reflection in a store window.

Alexander chuckled. "Are you ready, Frances?"

Jack turned to grin at Frances. But she was already nearly out the stable door.

"Don't forget to drop the button," she said over her shoulder. "If you don't, I won't know that you've managed to get inside the wagon." A moment later she was crossing Front Street, straightening the hat she had tied under her chin with a worn ribbon. "And you'd better be quick, too!"

"Excuse me, sir," Frances called out. "Where might I find Tenth Street?"

Rutherford Pratcherd stopped pacing and looked up from his boots. "You won't find it," he said. "The town only goes up to Seventh Street."

"Well . . ." Frances wanted to smack herself. It was one thing to ask for directions in New York. It was another thing to do it in a tiny Kansas town. "Well, of *course*. I was simply asking where I *might* find Tenth Street. Because . . . oh my goodness, look how your boots are *shining*. Are they *new*?"

Frances was trying her best to smile, to talk like Miss DeHaven when she wasn't being cruel, and to keep from looking over at the Pratcherds' black wagon, which stood waiting down the street. "I mean," she continued, "they look so fine and . . . *clean*."

"They sure are new," said Rutherford. He smiled and showed a row of teeth stained with tobacco. "Pleased to meet you. Uh, my name's Ford. Ford Pratcherd."

"Ford," Frances repeated. *Ford?* "What an exquisite name." She choked on a laugh and hoped Rutherford would think it was a coquettish giggle. "My name is . . . Amaryllis Vanderbilt."

Rutherford's eyes widened. "Vanderbilt? Any relation to those rich railroad folks?"

"Oh, they're cousins," she said distractedly as she walked up the sidewalk toward the wagon, peering at the ground.

"What are you looking for?" Rutherford asked.

"A button from one of my shoes," Frances said, lying. "I think I lost it somewhere around here."

"How long are you in town for, Miss Vanderbilt?" Rutherford was following her. "Might you have a calling card?"

Frances's mind raced as she tried to think of answers while scanning the ground for the button Jack was supposed to drop. "Why, I'll just be a few . . . I haven't any cards. . . . I . . . I *found it*!" There it was, the button, lying near the back wheel of the wagon. She grabbed it and straightened up. "Thank goodness," she said. "I'd better go get this sewn back on!"

Rutherford smirked. "You'd better. Ain't proper for a gal to lose buttons."

Frances's face was hot. *It's not proper to steal my little brother*, she thought with rage. But all she said was "It was *lovely* to meet you, *Ford*." She knew that Jack and Alexander were just a few feet away in the wagon, and she hoped they wouldn't start snickering.

"Likewise," Rutherford said as he climbed up to the buckboard of the wagon. He tipped his hat at Frances and flicked the reins, and then the wagon started off.

Jack peered out the back window of the wagon. He could see Frances back on the wooden sidewalk. She stood there for a moment before she pulled her coat around her shoulders and hurried away.

He nodded toward Alexander to silently indicate everything was going smoothly. They'd been relieved to find the back of the wagon empty when they crept inside. Their plan would be hard enough without having a passel of scared new arrivals from the orphan train to contend with.

Jack caught one last glimpse of Frances as she headed toward the alley. How did it feel to have to go back into the woods to wait for your brother? What if after all that waiting there was nothing? Then it would be just like when he lost Daniel, that awful falling feeling. *I won't let that happen, Frances,* he thought.

The wagon turned a corner, and then they were on a country road.

Alexander nudged him, his expression grim. "It's the road to the ranch," he whispered.

22.
RETURNING TO THE RANCH

The boys waited nearly an hour after the wagon had been unhitched. Rutherford had pulled the wagon into a shed, so Jack and Alexander sat in the darkness; they didn't dare talk or even whisper until they were certain it was safe. Once they climbed out of the wagon, Jack slowly pushed the heavy shed door open a bit and slipped out. Alexander followed.

They blinked in the daylight. *Where to now?* Jack wondered as he looked around. In front of him was a cluster of farm buildings with a barn and a yard. Behind him was a big house with a tower and fancy painted wood trim. And then there were fields in the distance. He could just make out a dozen or so figures dotting the dirt rows, slowly dragging rakes or crouched down with shovels. They moved so wearily that if Jack hadn't known about the ranch, he would never have thought they were children.

Was Harold among them? Jack squinted, looking for Harold's red hair.

"The bunkhouse is down there," Alexander said, pointing at a long, low ramshackle building. "That's where all the kids from the orphan trains wind up."

Jack turned to look at Alexander. "That's right— you've been here before. I almost forgot."

Alexander shook his head. "You never forget a place like this once you've had to live here." His shoulders had become hunched, Jack noticed, as if he wanted to draw himself down into a shell and hide. If it had taken all of Alexander's nerve just to escape this place, Jack thought, then it was all the more reason why they had to get Harold out.

"But never mind that," Alexander said. "Let's head for the bunkhouse." He turned and crept along the side of the wagon shed and motioned for Jack to follow. They peered around the corner of the shed to look for the Pratcherds, and when there was no sign of them, they dashed over to the barn and hid again. Then the boys made their way to the bunkhouse, where they stepped slowly along the back. One of the windows had only a flimsy bit of oilcloth keeping out the wind, and it allowed Jack and Alexander to climb inside.

The bunkhouse was empty and quiet. Jack looked up and down the rough wood bunks, each one with a gray wool blanket folded on top. He glanced over at Alexander, whose eyes met his gravely. One of these beds had been his.

And now one was Harold's, Jack realized with a shiver. Harold, who just the other day had been climbing trees in Wanderville.

"It's the working day now, so nobody's here," Alexander said. "But the farmhands—the grown-up ones—get a dinner break soon, and the kids come back to the bunkhouse yard for 'recreation.' Though when you're out in that beet field all morning, you don't exactly feel like playing kick-the-can."

Jack could only nod. This place was far worse than the factory on Baxter Street.

Just then, a bell clanged outside, and the boys retreated to a dim corner where they could wait and watch out the bunkhouse's open door.

They came straggling into the yard: boys who

were Jack's age, girls who were Frances's age, others as young as seven or eight. Their shoes were crusted with mud, the knees of the boys' trousers and the hems of the girls' skirts were filthy and wet, and their dusty faces were streaked where they'd perspired. Jack recognized Lorenzo, who had taken to walking with hunched shoulders instead of standing at his full height. One boy limped; others shuffled. They lined up to drink from the water pail or else leaned against the side of the bunkhouse or the other sheds.

Alexander watched them all intently, and when a lanky kid in a chambray shirt passed near the open door, he gave a low whistle. "Nicky!" Alexander called in a whisper.

The tall kid stopped and turned. "Alex?" he said incredulously. "You're back!"

An older girl rushed over just then. "We thought we'd never see you again!" she said. She turned and motioned to two other boys in the yard to come over. "This is the kid we were telling you about," she said in a low voice. "The one who escaped."

"What are you doing here?" Nicky asked Alexander. "Did you get caught?"

Alexander shook his head. "Nope. . . ."

Jack cut in. "But our friend did. Have you seen him?" He stepped closer to the doorway of the bunkhouse, where he could see out into the yard. "He's about seven, with red hair, and his name is Harold," he said. He spotted a group of younger boys, but Harold wasn't among them. His mouth was suddenly dry as chalk. What if they'd taken him somewhere else?

A small crowd of kids had gathered at the door. Jack could hear them whispering. "Who's Harold?" one of them said.

Someone grabbed Jack by the arm.

"You came!" It was Harold. Jack finally breathed again. Harold was all right—grimy and tear-streaked, but all right. He pulled on Jack's arm and then Alexander's. "You came to get me!"

"Good luck with that, Hair-red," said a voice that Jack had heard before. *Quentin*. Good old Quentin from the train. His nose was swollen, and with his bad lip he looked like some kind of bulldog. Well, a bulldog that had lost a fight with a bull.

Harold straightened up and glared at Quentin. "My friends don't need luck," he said. He turned to look up at Jack and Alexander. "Right?"

Jack looked up and saw at least a dozen faces waiting for him to answer. Some he recognized from the train. Others were ones he didn't know. So many of them were pale and shivering.

"Right," he said. "And here's what we're going to do. . . ."

23.
REMEMBER, CHILD, REMEMBER

Frances sat down on the creek bank and took out the bread that Alexander had found in town. The walk back to the ravine had felt like the longest trek in her life, but she was glad to be back in a place that felt familiar, even if it was deserted. She looked around as she ate in silence. The rope swing turned slowly by the big tree, and over in the hotel, the hammocks billowed in the light wind. Could you still call Wanderville a town if there was only one person?

Then again, Wanderville was the sort of place that you could see half in your mind and half for real. So Frances tried to see through the woods to a vision of New York that she remembered—Essex Street at first daylight on a Sunday, with the awnings folded down over the storefronts. Not an empty place, but one that was just waiting. Maybe Alexander had seen it the same way when he first came here.

That made her feel a little better. After all, she *was* waiting—Jack and Alexander would just be arriving at the ranch now, and if all went well, they'd be coming back with Harold tomorrow. Or perhaps the next day. Whatever happened, she would be here.

"And so will Wanderville," she said out loud. It felt good to say it, even if nobody was listening.

In the afternoon, she curled up in one of the hammocks, reading pages from her *Third Eclectic Reader* and watching the clouds cross overhead. She looked up at how the sky was outlined by the tree branches and noticed how it all sort of resembled a map, with patches of sky in jagged shapes like states or countries, and the boughs crisscrossing like rivers. It made her think about how far she and Harold had traveled in just a few days.

The tree-branch map began to blur, and Frances wiped her eyes. There were so many things she hadn't told her little brother yet. He'd remembered the aunt who had taken care of them until he was five, until she'd gone out on a November night and never returned. A neighboring family had taken them in for a while afterward, and after that, the uncle who drank gin. Frances had never told Harold that Aunt Mare was gone for good. And she had never told him that Aunt Mare was their mother.

You must call me your aunt, her mother had insisted years ago, when Harold was just a baby. *And I'll tell the landlord that you're orphaned kin. That way he'll take pity. He wouldn't be so kind if he knew the truth.*

It was a lie that served Frances well after she and Harold were abandoned. The simplest thing was to let her little brother—and the world—believe they were orphans. Better to have a dead mother you never knew than a mother who'd just disappeared.

Now she wasn't so sure.

She turned a page in her reader and came to a poem that she read to Harold sometimes:

> *Remember, child, remember,*
> *That God is in the sky;*
> *That he looks down on all we do*
> *With an ever-wakeful eye.*

Truthfully the verse used to frighten Harold a little, what with the talk of a big eye. But the meaning rang especially true to Frances now. That first day, after she and Jack and Harold had escaped from the train, the sky had been so huge, and all they could do was try to walk to wherever it ended, so it made sense that God was in the sky. It was near sunset now, and in the last light she read the whole poem aloud as a kind of prayer—a prayer that Jack and Alexander and Harold would be safe and return to Wanderville soon.

She lay awake in the dark after that for a long time. *What if they don't come back by tomorrow?* she wondered. *Or the next day?*

Just before she dropped off to sleep, her eyes flew back open and she took a deep breath. If they didn't come back, she realized, she knew what she had to do.

24.
TATER THURSDAY

Rutherford Pratcherd was up before dawn, lugging a steaming pail of boiled potatoes across the bunkhouse yard. When he reached the orphans' quarters, he didn't stop to knock. Instead, he planted his foot against the door (admiring, once again, the shiny new leather on his boots) and shoved it open.

"Time for feed!" he bellowed as he clomped into the bunkhouse. "Get in your places!" It was Tater Thursday, when the farmhand orphans received a meal before their morning jobs. Other days they worked first before they were given their victuals. "Keeps them from getting shiftless," Mr. Pratcherd liked to say.

Thus on Thursday mornings the children would form two lines along the row of bunks. Rutherford treated the occasion like a cursory inspection, and any kid who was found wanting—for wearing a dirty shirt, for instance, or for failing to clean under their fingernails—would get his potato last, when it was cold. Never mind that *everyone's* shirts and nails were dirty; the inspection was all up to Rutherford.

Now he walked the length of the bunkhouse. Lately the little grubs had taken to scrubbing their faces and hands with extra vigor on Thursdays, and it was getting harder to single one of them out. So Rutherford hadn't expected to see a kid standing right out in the middle of the floor, just waiting to be made an example. It was the new kid, a short grub with red hair, and he stood there blinking at Rutherford.

Rutherford grinned. "Clearly you ain't familiar with the way things are done around here," he barked. "You're to be washed up and in line! Now get in place! Get!"

Harold just shrugged and wiped his nose on his sleeve.

Rutherford's face changed. "Do you defy me?" He set down the potato pail and reached for the whip on his belt. He raised it slowly, savoring the threat. He moved to snap it. Except the whip caught on something and jerked his arm back. "Hey!"

Someone behind him yanked the whip from his hand. It was Alexander.

Then Rutherford doubled over from a blow to the gut. Jack's punch.

Jack stood with fists ready. In the plan he'd devised with Alexander's help, Harold was the bait, and Rutherford had bitten. The scrapping lessons Daniel had given him on Doyers Street had served him well.

The ranch owner's son coughed and stumbled. "You orphan trash!" he said between puffs.

Alexander pulled Harold over to a corner, grabbing the pail as he went. The other children had broken out of their lines. Some had stepped back in caution; others crept forward for a better look.

"Now's your chance!" Alexander shouted to them. "Why don't you show Rutherford what you think of him?" He grabbed a potato and hurled it at Rutherford. Lorenzo strode over, stood up straight and tall, and threw one, too. Then Nicky took up the pail and held it out for the rest of the kids. "Rutherford can have *all* the taters today!" he called out as the other kids cheered. He reached in the pail with one skinny arm, pulled out a warm potato, then pitched it hard.

"Quit it!" Rutherford hollered. At first he simply

ducked; then he started trying to catch the potatoes and throw them back at the orphans. "My pa's giving you all extra chores today!"

Jack didn't stop to throw a tater; instead he found Harold and nodded over to Alexander. Nearly a dozen of the young farmhands had backed Rutherford into a narrow spot between two bunks. Several were gathered around the pail, eating the last of the potatoes. All this commotion hadn't changed the fact that the kids were still hungry.

Alexander handed the whip to Nicky. "Take care of this," he told him. Then he joined Jack and Harold, and the three of them began to back slowly toward the end of the bunkhouse where the door was.

Jack went over the plan in his head: *Get Harold to a safe spot first.* Once they slipped out, the other kids were sure to notice, and maybe they could escape, too. How much time did they have? A few more steps, and they'd be at the door. It was still dark out, dark enough to run—

Just then the bunkhouse door banged open.

"Where's Hair-red going with his friends?" Quentin brayed.

In the doorway behind him was a massive figure with great big, round shoulders and a wide-brimmed hat. Alexander's face turned ashen as he recognized him, and Harold's eyes widened, too.

It was Mr. Pratcherd.

"Here they are," Quentin told Mr. Pratcherd proudly.

The ranch owner lifted his cane and used it to nudge Quentin aside. "You're back," he told Alexander, his voice a resonant growl. "We never forget the ungrateful ones who run away."

Jack and Harold shrank back, but Alexander squared his shoulders. "I came back to say thanks for nothing, you greedy snake!" he spat at Mr. Pratcherd.

Jack felt as if his heart would stop. Even Quentin sucked in his breath. Mr. Pratcherd glared at Alexander and banged his cane against the bunkhouse floor as he lurched toward them.

"Take Harold!" Alexander whispered. "You know where to go."

Jack thought quickly. *Where?* Suddenly he remembered: the back window of the bunkhouse, the one they'd used to get in. He nodded, then hesitated.

"Go!" hissed Alexander. "Never mind me!" Then he pitched himself in Mr. Pratcherd's direction, blocking his way.

"Move aside, boy!" the ranch owner yelled. He raised his cane again.

Jack reached for Harold's arm and pulled him along as he ran past the bunks. By now Rutherford had gotten control of the whip again, and he was snapping it to keep the children back.

Jack's mind raced. *Where's the window?* Finally, he found it—it would have been easy to miss; it was covered by a thick oilcloth and barely let in any light. "Come on," he told Harold as he pushed the oilcloth aside. He helped the younger boy climb through the window, then swung his leg over the windowsill to clamber out as well.

When Jack got outside, Harold was waiting.

Unfortunately, he wasn't alone.

Behind him stood Mrs. Pratcherd, wearing a dressing gown trimmed with black fur over a muddy pair of galoshes. Her hair was knotted up in rag curlers, in what seemed to Jack like a thousand scraps of muslin whose ends flicked in the wind like snake tails. She had a firm grip on Harold's shirt collar.

"We'd hate to see y'all leave the Pratcherd ranch," she said, her voice flat. "I think you'd best stay a while longer."

25.
To Tell
A Sad Story

Frances knelt at the creek bank and splashed her face. She winced at the icy cold of the water, but she reached in and doused her face again and again.

It was the third morning since Jack and Alexander had stowed away in the black wagon, and they hadn't come back with Harold. When there had been no sign of them at all by the end of the second day, Frances's thoughts began to run as fast as the creek rapids she listened to for hours at a time. Had the sheriff caught them on their way back from the ranch? If he had, then the law would have probably come looking for her, too. No, the boys must still be at the Pratcherds'.

It was time for Frances's plan, the one that had come to mind her first night alone in Wanderville. It was almost as if Aunt Mare herself had told her what to do. *Remember how it was on Hester Street?*

She splashed her face once more. The cold water was a ritual she'd performed almost as long as she could wash her own face. It hadn't been by choice at first, but by the time she got to the Children's Home, where hot water ran from the taps, she stuck by it. For sure it smarted sometimes, but that was just the lesson she taught herself every day—to do something hard, something that hurt a little, just for practice. And there were days when the practice sure came in handy.

Frances did one thing different today, though. After the cold water, she picked up a handful of dirt and threw that on her face, too.

On Front Street in Whitmore, she was careful not to walk past the mercantile lest she be recognized as a thief. Frances crossed to the other side of the street instead, looking all around as she went. It was near noon and the people of Whitmore were setting out on midday errands.

She studied the storefronts, trying to decide where she'd take *her* business. Obviously the mercantile was out of the question. The bakery? There were several women inside, but would they just take her for a beggar? She turned to check her reflection in the bank window: Her face was grimy, her hair matted, her skirt hem muddy and damp. Aunt Mare would've told her she looked just like Brooklyn Molly, who was famous down on Hester Street for singing the most sorrowful songs to draw a crowd on the sidewalk—a crowd of fellows whose pockets were ripe for picking. Well, Frances wouldn't be doing *that*, but she was taking a page from Molly's book just the same.

She turned back to scanning the street. She didn't want to risk the post office, because that was where they posted handbills about criminals, and Frances was one, sort of. Then again, it was where the most people were gathered at the moment, probably waiting for the mail delivery that had come on the train to be sorted. She steeled herself. The post office, then; that's where she would go.

Frances started to walk, and then her walk turned into a run. She stopped only to open the post office door, and then she hurtled inside. Nearly a dozen faces turned in her direction. Grown-ups, buttoned-up folks with proper hats and coats.

"Will someone tell me where I can find Sheriff

Routh?" she called out. "My brother . . . I think he's dead!"

The office went silent, save for a few whispers.

Frances took a deep breath before she went on. She'd had a bit of a knack getting people to listen to a sad story back in New York, but this was her most captive audience yet.

"I . . . I worked at the Pratcherd Ranch," she lied. "With all the other orphans. But I ran away because . . . because it's a cruel place."

A murmur went up among the crowd.

"Another runaway," Frances heard a man say.

"I heard it's true," a woman added. "They're quite unkind there."

A stout woman drew out a handkerchief and began twisting it in her hands. "What happened to your brother, girl?"

"I don't know," Frances said. "He was going to escape, too. He was going to meet me at the depot, and he was supposed to be here by now. But I think something's happened. . . ." Her thoughts raced as she continued to spin her story. "There are dogs guarding the ranch. Mean dogs . . . I think they got him."

The woman gasped, as did some of the others in the crowd. "You mean . . ."

"I fear he's been killed," Frances said.

Someone was trying to get through the crowd from the back of the room. The stout woman looked up to see who it was. "Clarissa," she called, "did you hear this child's story?"

The person who was apparently named Clarissa had made it through to the front of the crowd at last. She took off her hat. And then Frances saw who it was: Mrs. Routh.

"Yes," Mrs. Routh said. She looked stunned and pale. "I heard every word. I had no idea. . . ." She looked Frances up and down. Did she recognize her as one of the runaways from the train?

It didn't matter. Frances could tell that Mrs. Routh believed her, even if parts of her story were fibbed.

"Please!" Frances begged. She kept up her act. "I promise I'll go back to the ranch, and I won't try to escape again. But I need to know if . . . if my brother's been killed."

Mrs. Routh nodded. "I'll get my husband. We'll go out to the Pratcherds' and get to the bottom of this."

26.
ROCKS
AND HARD PLACES

The sun was high, and sweat ran down along Jack's nose whenever he bent down to pick up a rock. Harold trudged along a little ways behind him, picking up the stones Jack had missed. They had to slog through the entire beet field today, clearing rocks so the dirt could be plowed.

Behind Harold was Alexander, who stopped every few feet to dig out the biggest rocks. He'd pry them from the ground and heave them over to a wooden pallet pulled by Quentin. The pallet made a scraping noise as it dragged along the dirt. To Jack it sounded like the breathing of a very sick, old beast that needed to be put out of its misery.

But Jack would have to live with *his* own misery. Not since his brother's death had he felt so wretched.

Not only was Daniel gone now, but Jack's freedom was gone, too, and every day he had to see the other kids here being worked—and beaten down—like mules.

Quentin looked a wreck, with a black eye on his left side and a gruesome scab under his nose. When he'd found out about the scheme to free Harold, he'd tried to get in good with the Pratcherds by ratting out Jack and Alexander. But Mr. Pratcherd had been so steamed about Tater Thursday that he'd pummeled Quentin anyway.

Alexander had taken a beating as well from the Pratcherds. An even worse one—his bruised eye was nearly swollen shut, and one side of his face had a savage-looking scrape across it. Jack thought it had to hurt, but Alexander wore it stoically, and he seemed sort of proud of the shiner. "Just *one* black eye," he said. "So I'm in half mourning." Maybe he was a little crazy, but Jack had to admit that Alexander had become brave. This was a *real* fight now—not the imaginary sort of battle they'd thought up back in the woods—and Alexander was willing to face it.

"Big rock," Alexander called out. Jack had to walk back and help him dig it out. Quentin was supposed to help, too, but he usually just stood there catching his breath. Truthfully Quentin was the best one suited to lug the pallet, since he was built like an ox, so they were lucky that he was at least willing to pitch in where he was most useful. Or so Jack reasoned as he helped Alexander dig.

The big rock was the size of a muskmelon, and it wasn't easy to pry it out of the dirt—the plank Alexander used was too short and they hadn't any shovels. Jack braced his shoe against the side and tried to wiggle it.

"I wish we had that big spoon with us, the one that you and me and Frances shared," Harold said. "We could dig that thing out in no time."

"What spoon?" Quentin asked.

Alexander and Jack exchanged a look. "Oh, just a . . . pretend spoon," Alexander said quickly. "Right, Harold?"

Harold nodded. Jack managed to loosen the large rock with his foot, and he and Alexander hauled it over to the pallet. Then they went back to the smaller stones.

But Quentin didn't seem convinced. He picked up the towropes again and hauled them over his shoulders so that he could resume his dragging. But he had gone only a few more feet before he dropped the ropes again and turned around to face the others.

"You know I ain't called you Hair-red since the other morning," he said, looking toward Harold. "I won't anymore."

Harold smiled a tiny smile. "Thanks." Jack and Alexander nodded, too.

Quentin wiped at his sweaty forehead with his sleeve. "It's just that I've been thinking." He looked around, paying particular attention to the edge of the field where Rutherford paced back and forth. Then he leaned in and lowered his voice. "The way you two showed up to get Harold . . . it wasn't just to get him out of here."

Jack's eyes met with his. "What do you mean?"

"I mean, you were trying to get Harold back to a particular place," Quentin said. "A safe place. Right?"

Jack didn't know what to say, but Alexander spoke up.

"Yes," he said. "We know a place, all right."

Quentin's eyes got big. "Can I . . ." He took a quick breath. "Can I come with you?" He shot a sheepish glance in Harold's direction. Harold shrugged. He wasn't scared of the bully kid from the train anymore.

Jack looked at Alexander for confirmation. Alexander gave a nod.

"Wanderville is open to any child in need of freedom," Jack said. "No matter who they are."

"Or what they look like," Harold added.

Quentin's hand shot up, like a reflex to touch his misshapen lip. But then he brought it down again to show that he was smiling. "Thanks," he said, turning to Jack and Alexander.

"You're welcome," said Jack. "Only thing is, we don't know how we're going to get there. We have to get out of here first."

Alexander agreed. "I wish we had another idea."

"There's Frances . . . ," Harold began.

"But she's just one person," Jack said. "What can she do?"

"It's not like she can just come whisk us all away in a wagon or something," Alexander pointed out.

"You're not *listening*," Harold said. *"THERE'S FRANCES!"*

He pointed across the field to the bunkhouse yard.

There was Frances, shading her eyes with her hands and looking out toward the fields, though she hadn't spotted them yet.

"How did she get here?" Jack said. Something strange was happening, he realized. A wagon and two buggies had pulled up, and now a half-dozen adults were in the bunkhouse yard. He could see from here that one of them was Mrs. Routh.

"There's a whole passel of folks from town," said Quentin in amazement. "And the sheriff, too."

"The sheriff's here?" Alexander said, an edge of panic in his voice.

By now Harold was running across the field. "Frances!" he cried.

Frances saw them now, too.

"Harold!" She raced out to her little brother and held out her arms. "I got you," she whispered. As she hugged him tightly, she looked over at Jack and Alexander and grinned through her tears. "And we're going home."

27.
CITIZENS AGAINST PRATCHERDS

"Oh my gosh," Frances said when she saw the bruises on Alexander's and Quentin's faces. "What happened to you?"

"Nothing happened," said a voice behind them.

It was Mr. Pratcherd.

"You boys turn around and go back out to that field and get to work," he growled. "You hear me?"

"Now wait a minute!" Jack heard a woman exclaim. He turned and saw a stout lady marching out to the edge of the yard where they stood. She wobbled a bit as her delicate shoes sank into the dirt. She was followed by several others who had come from town, along with the sheriff and his wife.

Jack blinked in confusion and turned to Frances. "What's happening?" he whispered.

"Did you bring the whole town here?" Alexander asked incredulously.

"I . . . I think so!" Frances replied. "Well, *most* of the town." She never imagined she'd be grateful to see Whitmore, Kansas. But here was Whitmore—or rather, its people—gathering in the middle of this beet field.

"Nobody's going anywhere until we find out what's going on!" the stout woman insisted.

Jack looked around. Mrs. Pratcherd had joined her husband, and she stood with folded arms. "Just what's this about?" she said, glaring around at the small crowd of adults. "What's the meaning of your visit, Sheriff Routh?"

The sheriff held his palms out. "I'm just here to keep the peace. But it seems some folks in Whitmore have questions about the goings-on here at the ranch."

An older man in a gray coat, who appeared to be the husband of the stout woman, stepped forward. "This child"—he motioned to Frances—"had reason to believe that her brother was dead. That he was killed on these premises."

Mr. Pratcherd sniffed loudly. "You mean this girl

here? Never seen her. But clearly you busybodies can see that she's found her little brother alive and well."

"I suppose he must have gotten lost and wandered onto our property," Mrs. Pratcherd said. She simpered at Harold, who was holding Frances's hand. "Naughty boy, running away from your sister like that."

"Now wait a second," the sheriff said. "You mean this girl doesn't live and work on your farm?"

"No, and don't believe a word she says," Mr. Pratcherd said. "I don't know this little wastrel, and neither does my family." Rutherford had come out of the barn just then, and Mr. Pratcherd waved him over. "Do you know this girl, son?" he asked, pointing to Frances.

Rutherford's eyes lit up. "Miss Vanderbilt! What are you doing here?"

Mrs. Pratcherd shoved Rutherford so hard he stumbled. "Lying, that's what she's doing." Her eyes flashed in a rage.

"Actually, Mrs. Pratcherd," Mrs. Routh said suddenly, "I think *you've* been lying! Lying to me and to the Society for Children's Aid and Relief! I can't deny it anymore. You and your husband . . ."

"Clarissa!" the sheriff exclaimed. He cleared his throat. "Clarissa, you can't just *accuse* people. . . ."

"Virgil," Mrs. Routh said, "we need to talk. Alone."

"Excuse me," Sheriff Routh told everyone, a little sheepishly. "We'll be right back." He steered his wife away from the crowd and around the corner of a nearby shed.

For a moment nobody else spoke.

The other young farmhands had sensed that something strange was happening, and they'd crept out from the bunkhouse and in from the fields to watch the apparent standoff between the assorted townspeople and the Pratcherds.

As Jack watched the adults glaring at each other, he felt strangely invisible. Even when the grown-ups had been talking about Frances and Harold, they hardly even looked at them. Except for Rutherford, who stared curiously at Frances (probably still wondering if she was really a Vanderbilt), the crowd all but ignored the children. It seemed the adults were all busy playing some kind of game with one another where they pretended to be polite.

One of the women from town, a matronly lady with spectacles, broke the silence. "I do hope you understand why we're so concerned," she said in a syrupy voice to the Pratcherds. "It's just that there have been so many runaways lately, sneaking around town and stealing things."

"You can hardly blame us for that," Mrs. Pratcherd said coldly.

"Unless they're running away for a reason!" the stout woman broke in. "Just look at the bruises on those boys over there," she said, pointing at Alexander and Quentin. "What happened to *them*?"

A few of the women from town gasped to see them. Quentin grimaced, but Alexander nodded and pointed at his shiner.

"They did that to each other!" Mr. Pratcherd sputtered. "They're slum kids from New York. They're practically animals!"

"They're incorrigible!" Mrs. Pratcherd added. "They need to be reformed!"

Frances had to keep from grinning at the spectacle that was unfolding. It was better than any uproar that she'd ever seen raised on the Lower East Side. Just then, though, she felt Harold tugging at her sleeve. "What is it?" she said.

Harold motioned for her to crouch down, and he whispered something in her ear.

Meanwhile the adults continued to squabble. A man from town spoke up. "I think these little wretches need to be in a proper institution! Not running around our town like wild dogs."

"Not dogs!" cried another woman. "Innocent children!"

More voices joined in.

"They're little criminals, these children."

"Well, I think the folks running this ranch are the criminals!"

"Did you see that awful bunkhouse? Shameful!"

"Why don't you people mind your own business?"

The space between the townspeople and the Pratcherds had become smaller. They were closing in on each other even as their voices grew louder.

Jack turned to see what Frances thought of all this, but she wasn't there. Neither was Harold. Where were they? He spun around nervously, looking.

Alexander tapped Jack's shoulder. "Over there," he whispered.

Frances was waving from the doorway of the bunkhouse. Waving for them to come over.

Alexander slipped away from the crowd, followed by Jack, who pulled Quentin along, too. They kept their footsteps soft as they crept inside the bunkhouse.

"Look!" Frances exclaimed. She pulled away the oilcloth on the bunkhouse window, and Jack could see what she was so excited about. There, right behind the bunkhouse, was the black wagon.

28.
AN OPPORTUNITY PRESENTS ITSELF

"**N**ow's our chance," Frances whispered once the boys came over. "The wagon's already hitched, and the adults are all still in the yard."

Jack just gaped. "How did you know the wagon was back here? And what do you aim to do?"

"A little bird named Harold told me where it was," Frances said. She motioned to her brother, who was now petting one of the horses. "And it's how we're getting out of here."

"You can *drive a wagon*?" Alexander asked.

"A little," Frances replied. Truthfully all she'd ever done was hold the reins of the neighborhood rag peddler's cart whenever he'd needed a whiskey break. But it was better than nothing.

"I'll get my things," Quentin said. "Harold's, too."

Frances blinked in surprise. The creep who'd tormented her brother on the train was now his friend? But she could see from Quentin's face that he'd been through a lot since she'd last seen him. She nodded. "Hurry."

Quentin rushed over to his bunk and pulled his suitcase out from underneath. Meanwhile, Frances pulled herself up onto the windowsill to climb out.

"Wait," Jack said. "We need to take the others."

"You sure do," said a boy's voice from behind them. It was Lorenzo.

"I saw you run in here," he explained. "I figured you had a plan. I'll go get Nicky and Sarah and Fergus. . . ."

"Get everyone," Quentin said. "I'll help."

"So will I," said Alexander.

Jack held his breath as the other kids began to trickle into the bunkhouse, one at a time, to escape suspicion—though it didn't seem as if the grown-ups were likely to notice, seeing how their fighting had grown even louder. From the din of furious voices, Jack could only make out what Mr. Pratcherd was saying.

"Get off my property!" he bellowed. "Sheriff, arrest them for trespassing!"

Alexander and Lorenzo rushed back into the bunkhouse.

"Pratcherd's waving an old musket!" Lorenzo reported in a delighted whisper. "He says he's going to fire warning shots to make all the busybodies leave!"

"Mrs. Pratcherd's yelling at him and saying he'll scare the horses," Alexander added.

Jack grinned. "Did you round up everyone else?" So far there were four other kids in the bunkhouse waiting near the window with Frances. Jack had counted at least twenty-two young farmhands at the ranch. Were they all in on the plan yet?

"Quentin's getting the word out," Lorenzo said. "He and the others will meet us around the back."

"Perfect. Let's go."

One by one the escaping farmhands crept through the window and then into the back of the black wagon. First Lorenzo, followed by a younger boy, then two girls—one blond, the other with braids— then a skinny boy who was quick as a rabbit. Frances checked on Harold, making sure that he was safely in the back with the others, then crawled up front. Jack and Alexander waited outside the wagon.

"Where's Quentin and the other kids?" Jack

wondered. He and Alexander crept toward the corner of the bunkhouse listening for footsteps. Finally they heard the sound of running feet, and Quentin appeared.

"The sheriff's coming this way," Quentin told them, nearly out of breath.

"Looking for us?" Alexander asked.

"No," Quentin panted. "His wife. She made some kind of fuss and ran off. The rest of the other kids are in the bunkhouse waiting."

Jack thought quickly. "Let's get in the wagon and hide there until the coast is clear," he said. "Then we can get the last of the kids and go."

"Good idea," Quentin whispered. "I'll go back to the bunkhouse and tell them." He ran back in the direction of the yard, where the adults still argued.

Jack and Alexander hurried over to the wagon and climbed up to where Frances was sitting.

"Get down under the seat!" Jack told her. "We have to hide!"

Frances nodded, but her eyes were wide and frantic.

"What's wrong?" Jack asked.

"I just realized," Frances said, "I . . . I don't know how to start the horses."

"Don't worry about that yet," Alexander hissed. "Just get down and hide."

"But what if I—" Frances started to ask. She didn't finish her sentence, though, because just then, two things happened.

The first was a tremendous noise that went *BLAM*!

Mr. Pratcherd had fired his Civil War musket into the air.

Then the second thing: The horse team hitched to the black wagon screeched and thrashed their heads and stomped their feet, and then they began to run.

29
THE UNSTOPPABLE WAGON

The wagon took off with a fierce jerk that nearly pitched Frances and the boys off the front seat.

Frances scrambled to take the reins. "Whoa-oh!" she called to the horses.

"Wait!" Jack cried. "We're not ready!"

"Try . . . telling . . . horses . . . that!" Alexander gasped. He'd tried to stand up, but now he was swaying back and forth so precariously that his arms began to windmill and flail.

The reins were thrashing and Frances felt them yanking her like a puppet. "Stop! Halt!" In her peripheral vision she could see Alexander's desperate motions. Was he going to fall off? *He was going to fall off.*

"*Alex!*" Jack was braced against the seat, and he lunged forward as the wagon hit one hard ridge.

Thunk! His hand caught just the back of Alexander's shirt, and he tugged until his friend fell back down in the seat with a thud.

"They won't stop!" Frances cried. "I can steer the horses, but they're not stopping!"

"Just hold on!" Jack told her. Trying to turn the wagon at this speed would be too dangerous.

He and Alexander crouched down to get a better hold on their seats while Frances braced her feet against the front board. Jack could hear muffled, surprised shouts from the kids in back and hoped they were holding on, too.

"The horses won't slow down!" she yelled.

Jack twisted around to look back. He couldn't see the bunkhouse yard or the Pratcherds or the other adults. Had Quentin noticed what happened? Jack faced the front again and saw that they were approaching a set of gateposts that would take them beyond a split-rail fence.

"We've reached the main road!" Frances gasped. "We're leaving the ranch!"

"Then we'll go," Alexander told them. "Turn left and *go!*"

As they turned, the road became smoother and the horses picked up speed. Now Alexander decided to look behind the wagon. He knelt on the seat and peered over the long black roof of the wagon.

"Uh-oh," he called out. "Jack, look . . ."

Jack climbed up next to Alex and saw what he was seeing: Back by the ranch gate, two figures had dashed out onto the road. Two men—Jack couldn't exactly make out their features with the distance, but it looked like the sheriff and Mr. Pratcherd.

"They're on foot! They can't catch us," Jack shouted over the rattle of the wagon.

"But they saw which way we're going," Alexander yelled back. He was holding onto the edge of the wagon seat with one hand, and the other he held over his shiner to protect it from the road dust. He looked straight at Jack with his good eye. "We've got to get the wagon off the road."

"*How?*" Frances called up from her spot behind the reins. "We can't stop!"

The boys exchanged a nod. Jack turned back around and slid next to Frances on her left. Alexander took the spot to her right. "Who said anything about stopping?" he said.

Jack could see Frances's eyes grow wide, though she didn't dare take them off the road. "Right!" she said. "Just say when."

Jack scanned the side of the road for a good place to turn off—some place that wasn't too bumpy, or muddy, or fenced off—while Alexander crouched down to tap on the window that led to the back of the wagon.

"Attention, passengers!" he called through his cupped hands. "By and by there will be some jostling as we change our course. . . ."

"*Hold on!!!*" Frances screamed.

The horses surged to one side and yanked the wagon so hard that one side swung up, then down with a *slam* and three bumps so wild that Jack swore he felt his teeth rattle.

The noise beneath the wagon had changed—from the clatter of the hard road to a deeper pounding sound. They were driving over dirt, over grass, across the open prairie.

Frances nearly toppled out of her seat from shock. "We did it," she breathed. The boys clasped her shoulders on each side.

"Don't fall off now," Alexander said with a laugh. "Just keep driving until we get to the railroad tracks. And then we'll be almost home."

30.
ALMOST HOME

It turned out Frances didn't need to worry about stopping the horses. Once they'd reached the railroad embankment, which was too high for the wagon to cross, the horses simply slowed down and then stood in place.

Frances's legs felt like jelly as she and the boys raced around to the back of the wagon. "Harold!" she cried.

He was the first one to jump out. "I told everyone not to be scared," he said as his sister folded him into a hug.

"Were *you* scared?" Frances asked, keeping him close.

"Sure," Harold said matter-of-factly. "But I also told myself not to be scared. You always tell me, Frances, but I can tell myself, too."

"Yes," Frances whispered, hugging him once more. "Yes, you can, Harold." Then she let him go and watched as he ran back to the wagon to help the others climb out.

Jack was checking on the horses. "We have to ditch the wagon here because it'll be too hard to hide it by the creek," he called over to Frances. "It's a shame. . . . These seem like a fine team of horses."

"We really left Mr. Pratcherd and the sheriff in the dust, didn't we? They didn't have a chance of catching up with us," Frances said, stroking the horses' heads. "Thank you, whatever your names are," she told them.

"They saved the day," Jack said, though it didn't sound quite right to say those words. Not with Quentin back at the ranch still, with the other kids they hadn't rescued in time. Jack should have known the horses would bolt. He should have gotten more kids into the wagon before it took off. He looked out across the prairie.

Frances pointed west. "The Pratcherd place is out that way, if you're wondering," she told Jack. "And I've a feeling you *are* wondering."

"Do you think they're all right?" Jack asked. "Quentin and the others?"

"We won't forget about them, Jack," Frances said. "None of us will."

She went to help the other children who were clambering out the back of the wagon. Jack, meanwhile, stayed by the horses, staring out at the spot on the horizon where Frances had pointed.

Harold grabbed Frances's hand and pulled her over to meet the others from the ranch.

"Lorenzo and Sarah were on our train," Harold told her. "And here's Nicky, and George, and Anka."

Frances remembered dark-haired Lorenzo. Sarah looked close to her own age, and Frances had known her on the train not by name, but by her smooth braids and wry smile.

Nicky had black curly hair and was very skinny, and Alexander seemed glad to see him. "He was on my train," Alexander explained.

"Anka's ten and she's from Poland!" Harold told Frances. She had ash-blond hair and was shy to speak, but she looked strong and smart.

"I'm George," said the last boy, a towheaded kid who looked close to Harold's age. "Where are we going?"

"You'll see," Frances told him.

Alexander and Lorenzo helped Jack unhitch the team of horses. Once the horses were loose, they stepped up over the railroad embankment and trotted off down the other side.

"I think they know there's an oat field over that way," Alexander said. "They'll enjoy grazing."

Jack nodded in agreement, then motioned toward the wagon. "When the sheriff finds the wagon by the tracks, maybe he'll think we hopped a train."

"Let's hope so," said Lorenzo.

Soon they were all walking across the open prairie. Alexander was a few paces ahead of all the others, and Frances ran up to walk with him.

"I'm sorry I doubted you before," she told him quietly. "When we fought after Harold was taken." She looked up at his black eye. "I'm sure it wasn't easy to go back to the Pratcherds' after all you'd been through there. That was really brave of you. . . . Thank you."

"You're welcome," he replied. "And, uh, thanks for driving."

"Well, sort of driving." She laughed. "But you're welcome."

Jack recognized the lone tree where he and Frances and Harold had spent their first night in Kansas. It seemed like months ago now.

"We'll walk toward that tree and then head straight east," he told the others. "And then we'll be in Wanderville."

"Is that a town?" Sarah asked.

"Yes, in a way," Jack replied.

"It's *our* town," Frances said.

They reached the spot where the ground began to slope downward into the ravine.

"This way," Alexander said as he led them toward the creek.

Jack had wondered if Wanderville would be the same as he remembered. Not that it would have changed much in the last three days, but would he see it the same way? Would it still seem like their town, or just a rough campsite in the woods? And what would the others think of it?

But then he saw the little clearing and the creek bank and the fireplace. The courthouse, the hotel, and the storehouse. His tree and Frances's tree and Alexander's. And the stones Harold had arranged. It was all there.

The two girls and the three boys from the ranch walked slowly around the clearing, looking up at the trees and down at the creek. They said nothing, and the combined sounds of their footsteps moving through the dry leaves made a strangely restless noise.

"Welcome to Wanderville," Alexander said a little nervously. "Over here is the main square. . . ." But his voice trailed off.

"Just let them look around," Jack told him, his voice low.

Lorenzo walked over to the courthouse and nudged the big rock with his foot. Nicky was over by the hotel.

"Do you think they see it?" Harold whispered to Frances.

Frances watched for a few moments. "I think so," she said.

Sarah had found the rope swing. "Oh," she sighed. "This is the best thing ever."

George was walking along the log bench. He pointed to the rock wall. "Did you make this?" he called over to Harold.

"Yes!" Harold said, running to join him. "Let's keep building it."

Nicky had picked up the flint rock, and Alexander went over to show him how it worked. Lorenzo was scaling the big tree.

"This is excellent," he called down to everyone. "Excellent!"

Frances and Jack walked over to where Anka was standing, in the pine tree grove of the hotel. She was turning slowly all around.

"What do you think?" Jack asked her.

"I like very much," Anka said. "And I like this." She pointed to a fork in one of the trees where Frances had placed a short plank of wood just the day before. She had wedged it in firmly between two branches and made sure it was level so that it could be used as a shelf.

Anka reached into one of her pockets and pulled something out. It was a small doll, carved out of wood. The doll had a full wooden skirt like a little bell, and it was painted with stripes and dots and flowers. Anka put it on the shelf. "There," she said, and turned it so that Jack and Frances could see the doll's face. The head had a painted kerchief and a tiny smile and closed eyes that were like little smiles, too.

"There," she said again. It looked perfect.

31.
A TOWN THAT WANDERS

They decided they would build a bonfire at dusk, partly because they suddenly had a bounty of firewood—Nicky and Lorenzo had been practicing with the hatchet on a big fallen tree—and partly to celebrate the new citizens of Wanderville.

"There are nine of us now!" Alexander had declared while standing on the courthouse rock. "Our numbers are growing stronger."

Jack couldn't help but think that it would have been even better to have *ten*. Ten or more, with Quentin and the others. But he cheered with the group all the same. Then he went to start the fire while Alexander showed Anka and Sarah the pantry.

Frances looked around, suddenly on her own. Where had Harold gone?

She turned and at last spotted her brother by the creek, sitting on the bank with one of the new boys, George. They looked close in age, and Frances hoped they were becoming friends. She headed in their direction slowly, gathering sticks for kindling as she went.

"I never knew her," she heard George say. "She died when I was born. Then my da gave me up."

They were sharing their stories, Frances realized. Their orphan stories. Their backs were to her, and she ought not to be overhearing them. But then Harold spoke up.

"We had our aunt Mare," Harold said. "Only . . . she was really our mother. She once told me."

Frances stopped breathing for moment. *He knew.* When had Mare told him? Frances had no idea that he'd known.

"Why'd you call her your aunt?" George asked.

"Don't know. She told us to. I think it was because we didn't have no father." *Any* father, Frances wanted to correct him.

Harold turned around just then, as if he could hear her mind. "Isn't that right, Frances? About Aunt Mare?"

"Yes," she told him. "She thought it would be better if folks believed we were her orphaned niece and nephew." Their mother had just been trying to protect them, she realized. Just as Frances had wanted to protect Harold. But maybe the truth was just the truth, and it wouldn't hurt them anymore. Not here in Wanderville, at least.

"Anyway," Harold told George, "she went away when I was little. Right, Frances?"

Frances blinked her wet eyes and smiled. "Right."

"Don't cry, Frances," her brother said. "It was a long time ago."

"You're using the flint again instead of the matches," Alexander remarked, watching Jack struggle with the rock and the hatchet. "What's wrong?"

"Quentin," Jack said, hitting the flint. "The others at the ranch. The ones I didn't save." Like Daniel, he thought. Daniel, who needed his help that day in the factory. "I've got to do something."

The flint broke in two. Jack sat up and took a deep breath, then he went to pick up the pieces. But Alexander reached in and grabbed them instead.

"You mean *we*," he said. "*We* will do something to help the others. You and me and Frances."

"And Harold," Frances added. She had come over just then. "Don't forget about him."

Jack shook his head. "How could we—"

Frances interrupted, "He wouldn't be here if it weren't for you."

Jack looked up. "Really?"

"Neither would I," Frances said. She looked a bit like she'd been crying, but by now a grin had replaced her tears, her frizzy hair framing her beaming face.

"And neither would Wanderville," Alexander said. "Come on, let's start that fire."

For their supper, Jack and Anka cooked up a stew of canned beans and ham. George surprised them all by contributing two potatoes that he'd saved from the infamous Tater Thursday battle.

"I got deep pockets," he said.

They had to share dishes and pass them around the fire to eat the stew, but everyone agreed it was a thousand times better than the food on the ranch.

"Or those puny sandwiches on the train," Sarah said. "Frances, remember that horrid Miss DeHaven? With the sleeves?"

"She was on our train, too," Nicky said. "I heard she's Mrs. Pratcherd's sister."

"You mean monsters have sisters?" Lorenzo said, and they all laughed.

But Anka shuddered. "They are not good people, the Pratcherds," she said. "They will look for us."

"Yes, and Sheriff Routh, too," Jack pointed out.

"I wonder what Mrs. Routh thinks," Frances said. "I feel like she knows the Pratcherds are cruel to us and she's trying to tell her husband."

"But he's still the sheriff. His job isn't to care about us, just to keep the order," Jack replied. "Trouble is, we can't live on our own without being on the wrong side of the law."

"That's why we can't stay here forever," Frances sighed.

"I was thinking about California," Alexander said. "It's supposed to be better there. Warm and nice, and you can pick oranges by the side of the road. And see the ocean."

"You mean . . . leave Wanderville?" Jack asked.

Alexander grinned. "Of course not. Wanderville is here, right now. But it can be any place we want to be. Any place we build it."

"Can that be the third law of Wanderville?" Harold asked. "That it can be anywhere?"

"Sure!" Alexander laughed. "I mean... we hereby declare it!"

"It's a very good law," Frances agreed. Lorenzo nodded. "A town that wanders."

"Right," Alexander said. "It's anywhere we decide that we're better on our own, not pushed around or ignored or treated like stray animals. It's anywhere we can choose how we live."

"And it's anywhere we can help other kids, too," Jack added. "Where we can bring them and show them how life can really be." He took a deep breath. "Better than the ranch, or the Lower East Side, or . . . or sent off to live with strangers."

He stared out at the new faces around the fire. In some ways, they were *all* new faces—a month ago he hadn't even known Frances or Harold or Alexander. He hadn't any idea that there were towns in the middle of nowhere—towns on the prairie where the railroad took you, but also towns that you made yourself. Well, not just by yourself.

His eyes met Frances's and she smiled.

"It's where friends are," she said. "And there's room for more."

ACKNOWLEDGMENTS

I am so grateful for the amazing people at Razorbill—to Ben Schrank, who gave me the opportunity to build an imaginary town in the woods; to my editor, Gillian Levinson, for her thoroughness and energy that have inspired me both as a writer and as a fellow editor; and to everyone else at Razorbill who helped make this book happen. Thanks so much as well to Sarah Burnes, my agent, who provided encouragement and support; and to my husband, Chris, for reading my drafts and sitting with me to watch all the various documentaries and movies I sought out for research.

And special thanks to the staff and curators at the Old Courthouse Museum in Sioux Falls, South Dakota, for providing me with archived newspaper articles one September weekend when I first began writing this book in a hotel room and was desperate to know more about the children who traveled on orphan trains to the Midwest.

WANDER over to book two,
coming Fall 2014!

WENDY MCCLURE (WendyMcClure.net) is the author of *The Wilder Life: My Adventures in the Lost of World of Little House on the Prairie* and several other books for adults and children. She is a senior editor at Albert Whitman and Company, where her recent projects include books in the Boxcar Children series. She received an MFA from the Iowa Writer's Workshop and has been a contributor to the *New York Times Magazine* and *This American Life*. She lives in Chicago with her husband.